The Gaslight Adventures of Tom Turner

Gray's
ONE SHILLING

No. 2.

STORIES

Death
AND THE
Barbary Coast

BY T.E. MacArthur

GASLIGHT ADVENTURES BOOKS AND PUBLISHING

36, Dorset Street, Whitechapel, London

ALSO BY T.E. MACARTHUR

From TreasureLine Books & Publishing
The Volcano Lady: Volume I — A Fearful Storm Gathering
(2011)
The Volcano Lady: Volume II — To the Ending of the World
(2012)
The Yankee Must Die: Huaka'i Po (the Nightmarchers)
(2013)

Coming soon from TreasureLine Books & Publishing
The Yankee Must Die: Terror in the Wild Weird West
(Working title; late 2013)
The Volcano Lady: Volume III — The Great Earthquake
Machine (Working title; anticipated 2014)

From Q-werks Design
Shamanka: Oracle of the Shamaness (2008)

From The Tarot Media Company
Shamanka: Oracle of the Shamaness Guidebook (2011)

WORDS OF PRAISE FOR *THE VOLCANO LADY AND THE YANKEE MUST DIE*:

"A book is an adventure, something I have always said, and if you want a wild adventure, this is one well worth taking. The story is very delicately woven together to create a true masterpiece of fiction. Extra special treat with this novel, it is a stellar example of the Steampunk genre."
~ Penelope Anne Bartotto, Book Review Mama, *Library at the End of the Universe*

"MacArthur's research into the late 19th century is meticulous. She shows us manners, morals and mores while telling an entertaining tale that I honestly did not want to have end. I'm champing at the bit for Volume 2! Highly recommended for fans of science fiction, steampunk, gaslight romance and the tales of Jules Verne."
~ Sharon E. Cathcart, author of In the *Eye of the Beholder* and *You Had to be There*.

"What do you get when you take a believably science-minded woman-of-her-era (Victorian/Edwardian England) in an exciting story (Travel! Fashion! Early Feminism! Volcanoes!) and blend together with approximately a dozen Jules Verne characters and backstories? You get a book you don't want to put down... Well-crafted words and phrases echoed in my head every few chapters, and I had to pause and pull out of the story momentarily each time, to sit back and appreciate those moments. I rarely EVER do that, and I devour 50 or more fiction books every year."
~EAH, Reviewer

"Whoot! TE's newest installment in the Volcano Lady series is a wonderful homage to the penny dreadfuls with lots of intrigue and oh yes a cliffhanger... But for me the best part were the scenes in Kalakaua's Hawaii. And the fact that Madame Pele has a cameo is the icing on the cake. TE did a great job of bringing that time period back to life. Excellent read!!! "
~ Maryalice Tomoeda, Reviewer

THE YANKEE MUST DIE

THE GASLIGHT ADVENTURES OF TOM TURNER

DEATH AND THE BARBARY COAST

BY
T.E. MACARTHUR

The Yankee Must Die:
The Gaslight Adventures of Tom Turner
Death and the Barbary Coast
By T.E. MacArthur

©2013 by T.E. MacArthur
Edition 1.0 (2013)

Cover Artwork/Design: S. N. Jacobson
www.snjacobson.com

Published by: TreasureLine Publishing
www.TreasureLinePublishing.com

ISBN: 978-1-61752-158-4

Also available in eBook publication and paperback
www.volcanolady1.wordpress.com

Printed in the United States of America

Dedicated to my Mother and to my Papa as always.

Many thanks to Laura Ehrlich, Brandy Sluss, and Sharon Cathcart for their opinions, formatting, and editing skills – along with quite a bit of cheerleading!

To Gene Forrer who not only lent his name to a character but provided me with an enormous amount of historical data regarding airships and dirigibles – something I couldn't do without.

To Monsieur Jules Verne, the Father of Science Fiction (and Steampunk!)

Many thanks to the bewildering number of people who kept me sane and on track: Alex MacIver; Roy Nonomura; Jay Davis; Juliana and Patrick Gaul; Karin MacKechnie and Adam Lid; James Faraday; Margie Burke; Penelope Dreadful; Karen Krebser; Jaimey Grant; Anastasia Haysler, and Sonya Sutton.

To my writer pals Maggie Secara, Dre Sergent, Jay and Denisen Hartlove, Scott Perkins (AND the lovely Kristin Perkins,) Joel Reid, and James McShane; Molly Burke (the Queen of Confidence); Dennis Kytasaari; Penelope Anne Bartotto (the Book Review Mama herself); and David Batzloff.

To the continuing and inspiring resources: the U.S. Naval Landing Party (Civil War Naval Reenactors) and the North American Jules Verne Society (NAJVS.)

To the wonderful members of the Steam Federation – Bay Area Steampunk Association.

To the designer of the cover: Stephen Jacobson (www.snjacobson.com).

To Linda Boulanger and the gang at TreasureLine Books and Publishing

Freezing water – a cruel death at best.

The lid of his sinking coffin defied his desperate attempt to escape.

The coffin itself was sliding slowly down the muddy incline, sticking only long enough to promise hope before dropping again into the flood pool waiting at the bottom.

His fists struck the inside of the lid again, but the cold was weakening him.

The lid did not move.

Then, for a torturous moment, the coffin ceased its descent.

The Turner Luck?

His breathing slowed, by force of will. Waiting. Waiting. Every noise ringing in his ears, every movement of the wind exaggerated, his skin sensitive to every stimulation real or imagined. Waiting. Afraid to move in case he would shake the coffin and start it slipping again. Slowly, his sense of reality expanded beyond the bruises on his fists.

Tom Turner knew terror all too well. He'd known it at Andersonville Prison Camp, when the platform had dropped from under his feet and nothing held him but an old rope around his neck.

He began shaking in anger and sheer frustration; caught in the terrible vision of finally dying – suffocated at last. Death had been chasing him and now had caught up. His fingertips went numb. So too did his legs. His lungs burned. There was little difference between this and being strangled … hanged …

… It was over …

His life … oh God what a life he'd led …

… It was over …

November 1883 (Four months earlier)
Pier One, Central Embarcadero Wharf
San Francisco, California

"You should come back aboard," Commander Alexander Ehrlich said with as little emotion as possible. He didn't even look at Turner, but stood with his hands neatly clasped behind him and stared out on a town barely staggering to its feet in a fog hazed morning.

Ships in rows rocked and swayed in the wind, thumping up against the docksides. Bells rang and pulleys whined with each tug. A tangle of lines and masts cluttered the scene, while seagulls darted in and out of the rigging, squawking with irritation. A paddle-wheeler headed for Sacramento was building up steam pressure and her stacks hissed in protest. "Paddies" began their work excavating the last remnants of mudflats before the pile drivers could come in and start the foundations for another building where a marsh once lingered. The *U.S.S. Abraham Lincoln* was afforded a place of honor on the wharf at the end of Market Street which left her surrounded by vessels of every nation and trade. Passengers on the pier next to the *Lincoln* were beginning to queue up to board the ferry *The Capital* for her first daily run up to Sacramento.

"Mr. Forrer could certainly appreciate the company," he finally said when Turner remained silent.

Tom Turner looked down at the dock and his scuffed boots, smiled, and shook his head. "I'm too long out of class, sir. I'm the old dog who won't learn new tricks."

Ehrlich shot him a rather harsh glance. "Excuses, Mr. Turner. You're a sailor no matter how you try not to be. You belong on a ship – an American ship. I don't like the idea of a capable, American naval officer out of employment."

"With all respect, sir, you don't like the idea of a man with my background and skills not reporting to an authority you prefer." Ehrlich was clearly not used to backtalk. "And I don't blame you, sir. It was never my choice to leave the service. Now, I fear, I have lost any opportunities for my return. I'm flattered that you think such an option might yet exist."

Finally, with some exasperation usually saved for the newest ensign, Ehrlich faced his odd, civilian passenger. "Listen here, Turner. There is a place for every good man. Some are obvious, some are not. I have connections..." He paused as Turner's expression changed from casual to defensive. "Damn it, I know people in the right places. All you need do is be open to the possibility. Come back into service ... for your country."

Slowly, Turner's face slid into a frown. "I may have gone too far from home for that. I would not wish you to waste such connections or favors on someone as objectionable as me. But I mean this truly, I am flattered."

"I'm not flattering you! I'm being practical." The wind whipped up and raced through the sails behind them as they stood in awkward silence. Creaking wood and clanging metal quickly followed, and the same breeze lifted sections of Ehrlich's dark hair. He seemed not to notice.

Ahead of them, the fog cleared enough to show a wide avenue, traversed by carts, pedestrians, rail-bound trolleys, and bordered with grand, elegant buildings. Jutting off toward the right was California Street, busy and fancy as Market. Somewhere in the distance was the infamous Barbary Coast, as dirty and dangerous as it had been in its heyday of the 1850s.

"How is Forrer? You said your goodbyes didn't you?"

"Aye, sir. He's complaining about the lack of exercise."

"He would be dead if it were not for you."

Turner shook his head again. "A bit too generous of you, sir. He would never have been endangered were it not for me."

"Perhaps. Then again, it is a professional sailor's life, isn't it, to be in danger?" Ehrlich offered his hand, which by the slight gracelessness was not a normal gesture on his part, and waited to see if Turner would accept it.

The two men tried to pop each other's knuckles between grip and shake, like school boys sizing each other up at their first meeting.

Ehrlich tilted his head to the side slightly as though it would give him a new vantage on Turner. "Would you know an opportunity if it should arise?"

November 1883
The Royal Albert Hall
London, England

Lettie Gantry sat back, allowing a shadow to protect her from the notoriously vicious prying eyes of a judging public. And from particular eyes she did not want staring at her. She was satisfied that *they* knew where she was and not doing the very thing *they* told her not to do, under threat of severe punishment. Everything she did now was in public so that *they* could follow her every movement. It was what she endured to protect herself, her family and friends, and Mr. Turner – if he was still alive. Lord of Mercy, she thought, saving Mr. Turner and besting *them* at *their* own game was becoming an obsession. Perhaps ... no, very likely an unhealthy obsession.

The crowded symphony hall was beginning to quiet down at last. Until the members of the orchestra had started their preparations, the noise in the room had been quite unbearable, along with the temperature. The end of October and the start of November had been oppressively hot and the packed seats made things worse. Add to it the newly arrived rain storm more common to the time of year and the hall was stifling. She'd worn the best gown she owned for an evening performance and was roasting in the heavy, bronze-colored satin. Her black hair was up in a stylish way and her face was ever-so lightly powdered, though not so that anyone could tell. As her anxiety rose, she fidgeted with the old bead bracelet she'd kept for years and treated as an impious rosary. She would have worn something else, something she had worn in the tropical heat of the Dutch East Indies the summer before, but her luggage had not yet arrived in England. Her journey back via the Reuters Heavy Hauler dirigibles had limited her baggage but it had saved her three weeks of travel time, and ultimately brought her home well ahead of *them*.

It had likely cost Christopher Moore, her dearest friend and academic colleague, an extraordinary sum to purchase seats amongst the Loggia Boxes above the gallery near the orchestra. She would need to find a way to thank him. Of course, she had confided in him her goal of appearing to be "disinterested" in the life or death of Tom Turner. Moore used it as an excuse to indulge in his own love of intrigue, music, and William. He was mildly amused and shocked that she had taken such an interest in any man, let alone a wild American sailor.

The seats in the Loggia were quite plush and acceptably comfortable. Heavily upholstered in red velvet and set in pairs of two, the seats were coveted by many. Rich curtains hung from either side, and while kept clean they maintained that tell-tale scent of being in a room lit by hundreds of gas lamps.

"Any chance your 'Elegant Man' is out there?" Moore handed her a pair of silver and mother-of-pearl opera glasses. "If he is, I have some choice words to give him regarding that threat he made to you."

"You'd make a scene. Besides, recall that he was quite clear in his threat: I am not to contact or even consider Mr. Thomas Turner. The consequences would be … significant. And I am certain he has more than enough resources to make his threat real." Slowly, deliberately, Lettie raised the glasses and scanned the whole gallery as many of the social climbers and watchers did. The hall was a quite astonishing feat of architectural daring, but ornate plasterwork and gilding were not making an impression on her tonight. Even the fabulous organ, dominating the hall from behind the orchestra, could not hold her interest.

Where would the Elegant Man sit? He would have the funds to afford most any seat in the place, for who would do what the Elegant Man did for pennies? Yes, his employer paid him well, no doubt. He would be dapper in costume. Tall, rail-thin, dark haired. Bearded. Gold spectacles. And a cane. She remembered the cane. Anything so lovely, so unique, would be constantly in the hands of the gentleman who owned it. So, where would he be?

In the box next to them, a voice carried above the hushing crowd. "Watson, I have always preferred the relative intimacy of St. James Hall."

"'Intimacy?' St. James is huge."

"'Relative intimacy,' Watson. Relative." The voice quieted a bit. "But I must compliment you here."

"Well happy birthday, old cock," the other voice replied. "You deserve it."

Lettie leaned over to Moore. "Should we wish him a good birthday," she said with some humor. It was a bit vulgar for anyone to be heard in the box next to one, but under the circumstances, perhaps such a faux pas could be forgiven.

Moore carefully leaned back to William, who by propriety could not sit next to Moore and was exiled to the second set of seats. An annoyance to be sure, but the general populace had no understanding of what was between Moore and William – and no business knowing either. He wanted nothing greater than to reach out and to hold William's hand. It was not to be: they maintained that social mandate for secrecy. While Lettie never said a word on the matter itself, and always seemed to be perfectly comfortable with their relationship, she too could do nothing that would lack propriety. She understood the damage even a rumor could cause to either of the men.

Noting Moore's interest, William then leaned back so that he could see into the other box through the doors. "Say, there's some luck. That's the fellow from the newspapers." Lettie held up her fan so that William could speak with both of them privately. "A bit rambunctious if you hear it from his professors, but he's got a certain knack for working out puzzles in rather cold, logical terms."

"Haughtiness combined with pugilism is never a virtue to professors – trust me," she said with a wink. "How do you know so much?"

"Read it in the Times. Solved some case that had baffled the police for weeks. Fought off the criminals by himself. He's some sort of policeman, but not a policeman. Anyway, a well connected chap who just finished his studies, came home and found himself right pop in the middle of some horrible abduction – someone's wife. Oh, do stop me if I'm bringing you back any bad memories, Lettie dear."

"Not at all. You're such a dear: I'm quite recovered from the whole ordeal in Java. Did the police or this fighting logistician ever find her?"

"That's the thing, the police couldn't. So this fellow - can't remember his name, I have the paper at home so I'll get it - he solved it. He found the lady where no one else would have looked – in America! And he never left London. There's some good luck, and a resource or two. Left the police staggering from their failure. Apparently he uses some odd methods, but I say they're just scientific and if the police would use solid reasoning – wait - Holmes - that was his name."

Applause rose from the front of the hall and quickly was taken up by everyone. The conductor had arrived and was taking a cursory bow.

""'Holmes?' Are you sure?" Lettie picked up her fan immediately after she stopped clapping.

"Definitely. Something odd for a Christian name, but the family name was Holmes. A Consulting Detective. The name of the woman who was kidnapped never made it to the newspapers, so I presume this Holmes fellow kept it all hush-hush. Good show on that, I say."

"Rather decent I daresay. Trust me, being known as a victim is not what one wishes." Her mind wandered over to the other box. A *Detective*? She wondered if that meant what it sounded like it meant? Discreet too? Has resources and logic at his disposal? She wondered, with an odd sensation of pleasure, if the Turner Luck had rubbed off on her.

As the orchestra brightened the hall with a Strauss polka, *Die Emancipierte* – the Emancipated Woman – Lettie tried not to laugh. How oddly appropriate. William giggled a bit and Moore just shook his head.

Almost immediately she felt her mind floating along with the strong tempo. An excellent piece to begin with – it would set the feel for the rest of the concert. It was such an excellent choice that she allowed her thoughts to wander into a fantasy – which of course depended on whether Mr. Turner could dance. He had been an officer, so no doubt he could, though surely he was a little out of practice. She could hardly be one to complain if he was a bit off as she hadn't had a waltz or mazurka in ages.

Her mood plunged as she quickly inspected the crowds again below her box.

The Elegant Man rested his hands on his unique cane and glanced her way, with a dreadful smile.

The Berringer Hotel was several important things: cheap, central, and invisible. It was not, however, a proper hotel. The door was not in the front, but on the side of a dilapidated building, up a flight of dark stairs in the narrowest of alleys, shadowing its residents in appropriate shame for their lack of social attainment. The craggy-faced owner didn't care what Turner's name was, didn't really look at him, took the money, pointed up another flight of stairs, and mumbled something about the second door on the right.

The place was gloomy and only made worse by the gray clouds that had mixed with the fog, threatening to become rain in a climatic act of procrastination. It was unlikely to happen.

The room itself was nominally larger than the quarters he'd had on the airship *Albatross*, which was to say not very big at all. For a land-based accommodation, it was regrettably small, but one did not have a great expectation of what 50 cents a night could purchase.

Compared to what he was used to, for Turner, it was more than enough. All he had was in one duffle bag or in his pockets. As for money, he had a voucher from the Dutch government for 50 dollars, the money given to each foreign survivor of the Krakatoa eruption, and meant to pay for passage back whatever home they came from. The Dutch had enough on their dockets with their own citizenry in distress not to have to deal with people from other countries. It was far easier and cheaper to provide foreigners an impetus to go away. Turner had been classified as a tourist and given the minimum amount required to send him off sightseeing somewhere else, never mind his injuries.

Factually, this was not some great expense to the government or charities as there were not as many foreigners to chase away by Krakatoa's eruption as one might have thought. It was still charity. He wanted to be giving not taking. But, his choices were bare.

Lieutenant Albert Forrer had insisted on giving him some funds, going so far as to secretly slip it into his bag after Turner had insistently refused it – he found it while retrieving the few coins he thought he had. The hat Turner wore was an old fisherman's cap, and not the beautiful Homburg he'd bought in Paris the year before.

He was not quite the same man he'd been even a year ago. Then, he'd been self sufficient, able to acquire what he desired, to plan and to hope. So what if he had to do things that weren't precisely ethical? The overarching goal justified the means of achieving it – or so he told himself year after year, until experience and undeniable proof proved otherwise.

Life had taken its toll. He stared into what passed for a mirror over the wash bowl and noted the increased number of gray hairs on his head and in his scruffy beard. In fact, he looked the part of the down-on-his-luck loafer and drifter. That would have to change, but not immediately. He needed to be invisible for the time being and the luckless always go unseen.

Every smell or peeling bit of wallpaper reminded him of the years after the war, when ninety percent of the soldiers and sailors were turned out into the world with neither funds nor possibility. He'd learned to use his wartime skills to steal what he needed. There it was. He took from others and the shame was hard to accept. He'd done the only thing left, when small carpentry and road work dried up. He'd not gone yet to the railroads as too many out-of-work Confederates had done. One had to have money and connections to find employment there, and Turner had neither. Of course, there was the true reason: too many ex-Confederates.

Then there was the Wirz trial. He'd been obsessed with revenging himself on Henry Wirz, the commandant in charge of Andersonville Prison – the man who had him hanged. The man who gave him the scar. He'd always considered himself lucky in a freakish way: he'd not suffered nearly as much as others in the prison pens, exposed to the weather and wicked men from both sides of the war who preyed on the captured soldiers. Wirz had to pay for all the death, disease, starvation, murder ...

God in Heaven, were it not for the troops under Sherman, no man would have made it out alive. If only he had met Sherman and thanked him for what he'd done. The old general was Turner's hero and, no matter how many tales of Sherman's flawed character he heard, he always returned to his feelings of obligation and admiration.

Turner sat down heavily on the squeaky bed. He was lucky the straw mattress was on a frame and not on the floor. A pair of used blankets was draped carelessly over the end rail, and the pillow looked so hideous, he swept it from the bed without bothering to notice where it landed. His days of poverty had returned. The feeling weighed on his chest and made it difficult to breathe for a time.

From inside his waistcoat, he withdrew a neatly wrapped item that despite its overall bulk was easily hidden under his ill-fitting clothing. The object was surrounded in oilskin cloth, which had protected it from weather and water. Inside was a narrow journal, a little stub of a pencil, and a letter. *Her letter.* The one she made sure he would read on his voyage home. Where Dr. Lettie Gantry told him she could not spend the rest of her life with him. Where she promised she would not forget him either. Lettie had even gone so far as to sign her Christian name, which for a proper British lady was unheard of.

She would be ashamed of him, seeing him sitting there in his shabby room. This was not why she had placed him on board the *Lincoln*; not where she had intended him to end up.

Her kindness was familiar and its naivety anticipated. What did she expect to happen? That he would arrive in San Francisco to a cheering crowd and a grateful government? Actually, he'd half expected to disembark from the *Lincoln* straight into the arms of waiting government agents. The fact that he was not sitting in a jail cell still astonished him … and motivated him. As the sole survivor of the magnificent and extraordinary airship *Albatross,* and the only man still alive who could describe her inner workings, Turner knew he had a value to governments and weapons mongers alike. Never mind French intelligencer Pierre Jules Hetzel and his half-machine minions; anyone who had ever heard of Robur the Conqueror or the *Albatross* would want those many secrets.

Poor Lettie. She genuinely must have believed he would be quickly forgiven his former sins and allowed back into American society. Her reasoning was flawless based on the information she had; she simply didn't know the whole story.

His hands, still clutching the letter, were getting cold. The fog was rolling in and covering the city with a damp, soggy blanket.

It was possible that she believed he would simply change his name and disappear. That was the best plan actually. Doing that now would take skill and cunning. Hetzel was after him: Turner knew too much about the Parisian, his secret work for the French government, his intrusion into international affairs, and his use of mechanics to repair damaged human bodies. Hetzel was himself one of the "enhanced;" part automaton. Assassins in Hetzel's employ had already made several attempts on Turner's life – obviously not succeeding, he thought with a lopsided grin.

For all he knew of multi-national politics and ambitions, mad inventions, and far more insane inventors, here he was, sitting on a straw mattress, with little money, no friends, in a squalid hotel room. He'd come full circle – back to poverty.

No. He would not let it happen again. Commander Ehrlich's kind offer was only that … kind. It couldn't have merit despite its honorable intention. The government of the United States couldn't possibly view him as anything less than a danger despite his subtle loyalty. He would have to emerge from this on his own.

Of the fifty dollars, he could set aside twenty for transportation: either back to Hawaii or up to the Alaska gold fields. He'd have to labor on the ship as even twenty dollars wasn't enough for a regular passenger ticket, but that was fine. Ten more would buy him a respectable though inexpensive suit from one of the bespoke or department stores – there would be times he'd need to appear better off than he was. The rest would be necessary for food, rent, and possibly a newspaper now and then.

Lieutenant Forrer had given him twenty five dollars. It was a large sum for a Lieutenant making one hundred dollars a month and Turner could never pay the man back. He stubbornly couldn't use Forrer's money for avoiding poverty - that somehow didn't seem right. But he could use it for a wise purchase even Forrer couldn't disagree with. In the morning, after he'd washed and shaved, cashed the voucher and set about trying to make himself appear acceptable, he would find a gun maker.

Guns were easy enough to be had. One could purchase them at the same department store a man could purchase his shoes. But the clerks would ask questions in those fine stores. And the price would be higher than he could pay comfortably. No, a back-alley seller would have a selection at a price he could afford and with absolutely no interest in where the weapon came from or where it was going.

11

And, he was looking for something quite specific that no catalogue or store would carry for the average gentleman.

Turner wouldn't undress before falling asleep. He needed to be ready to move … to fight … to flee if needed. He used the duffle bag as a pillow, keeping it close. Hetzel was still out there with an army of men and machines. So far, he'd fought Hetzel's mechanical monstrosities and won. On the defensive. No difference in time or place was going to change the fact that Hetzel wanted his knowledge or wanted him dead. But there was one thing *he* could change: he would go on the offensive.

Late November 1883
41 Triton Street
Borough of Camden, London, England

The envelope stated very clearly: *Extremely Sensitive Matter.*

John Watson couldn't decide which would annoy his friend more, another inquiry or the fact that their new lodgings were owned and thus controlled by an elderly woman who already required too many rules. He was more curious about the new letter.

Extremely Sensitive Matter.

On the 13th of November, the letter arrived by evening post. It had initially been placed under a stack of important correspondence that included a signed lease agreement for set of rooms over on Baker Street, a slew of congratulatory messages to Holmes, and a bewildering number of inquiries regarding his trade and fees. Holmes scoffed, and with a sharp sniff dismissed all but the lease as being beneath a gentleman. A gentleman did not have fees, he informed the already well-informed Watson, and said gentleman chose which persons he would conduct his business with. "What is this world coming to?"

Choosing to ignore the inconsiderate slight, for Watson was a doctor who billed his patients, Watson slipped the newest letter off the pile which Holmes was on the verge of casting into the fireplace. It wasn't the first time his new friend had trod over his sensibilities. It was not in Holmes' nature to be aware of such trifles. And the very idea that he, a former Army surgeon, might become embroiled in the man's latest adventures was worth any momentary hurt feelings.

In his opinion, his friend Sherlock Holmes was a child in a man's body with a genius's brain. University classes had not really prepared him for the demands of social life. Holmes was well trained in mathematics, physics, and any other manner of science, most disastrously chemistry. His ability to reason had left his professors stunned. Yet, outside of academia, the work-a-day world had not provided him with the skills needed to be socially functional. Still,

Holmes was not *purposely* cruel; he lacked that in his nature.

"Did I step on your nerves, Doctor?" Holmes did not look up from his position at the mantle. He never looked anyone in the eyes when he knew he'd mis-stepped.

"Never you mind that, old cock. I think you can make it up to me with this." He held up the *Extremely Sensitive Matter* and mentally noted the slight but definite improvement in Holmes's behavior.

"What do you make of it, Watson? Come now; show me what you've learned." He stepped over several crates of books, awaiting the laborers who would collect them later that day and deliver them to the new residence.

Holding the unopened letter in both hands, the Doctor took a deep breath. Friendship aside, he was never certain if Holmes was asking out of interest or a need to make him feel a bit smaller. It was the negative side of being friends with a man who had a sense of self-importance bigger than Westminster Abbey and absolutely no self-esteem to support it. Very much a child. "This is very good paper, Holmes. I'd say it came from a set: envelope and sheet, matching. Extremely smooth and high quality. That would make it fairly costly. A very analytical hand," he noted, pointing to the meticulously written address. "Not a woman's hand, I think. A gentleman's. It is very practical and without much flourish."

Watson pushed the letter over toward his friend and leaned back on the sofa. He'd learned to be patient and not to expect immediate compliments – if any were to come at all. He had all the time he wished. He'd dressed to go out in the latest sack suit in oatmeal colored tweed. Proper attire for a man with a day to himself. No patients, no appointments. Leisure. He needed to be out of the way when the men came to remove his belongings, the few of them he had, to the other side of the city. His old leg wound was aching, but then it always did when rain was coming.

Holmes was rather the opposite. He had hardly risen from bed when the post arrived. He hadn't yet gone beyond his shirt, trousers, and dressing gown. He'd not even bothered to comb his hair. It was annoying at best. Bare feet were jammed into a pair of old Persian slippers which Watson had threatened to re-designate as a tobacco holder if Holmes didn't stop misplacing every ounce of tobacco they had.

Homes closed his eyes for a moment, ignoring that his black

hair was draped down into his face in an unkempt manner. Accepting the letter, he swept it under his nose. "An academic. Very likely a tenured professor of some years, as he is able to afford a luxury such as this. He has a wife who wears perfume; excellent perfume. Again, expensive."

"You didn't warn me that this was an exercise in olfactory detection." That would get Holmes's blood going.

Holmes sighed loudly and dramatically. "Use everything Watson, every time you observe. All five senses. Detection is a matter of collecting that which is commonly seen and most especially that which no one seems to notice. Such as scent."

"This is where I am to ask; Holmes old boy, however did you come to that conclusion? May we just assume the question."

Holmes laughed softly under his breath. "There is a slight aroma of French perfume and chalk. See here," he pointed to the letter, "a shiny spot on the envelope where the writer rested his hand while addressing it." He scratched at the surface and a light, white powder fell off. "A common teacher does not earn enough for this, as you rightfully described, quality set of papers. It is French paper: note the watermark near the point of the fold. Yes, a well placed professor, with connections in France or at least the good taste to make purchases while there. It could also be a scientist, but rarely do they find employment necessary for such fripperies."

Watson smiled, amused that he still found the inner workings of his friend's mind stimulating. "Well, open the damned thing, and let's see."

The inside sheet of paper did indeed match perfectly with the envelope, but the handwriting, while still analytical, was much less tidy. "Hurried. This letter was written in haste," Holmes said, scanning over the words.

"What does it say?"

Mr. Holmes. I wish to discuss with you a most urgent concern. Without meaning to sound dramatic, this is indeed a matter of a man's life. I will be in London and will call at 10am on the16th. I thank you for your consideration and sensitivity regarding privacy in this matter.

Watson's face screwed up, rubbing his new, thin moustache. "It sounds rather urgent, so why wait such a long time? That's two days from now."

"'I will be in London.' That's the key, Watson. This

professor, we shall call him that for now, is making a routine trip to London and will make specific arrangements to come to see us. He does not wish anyone to know, 'sensitivity regarding privacy' he said, thus he is concealing his visit within a regular trip into the city." He walked over to the fireplace mantel, rested his elbow on it and his chin upon his arm, and closed his eyes. "Still not enough information, Watson. I can hardly be expected to judge its veracity or significance without data." He was annoyed and now more likely to refuse the case.

For a long time they said nothing. Watson leaned over and picked up the envelope from where Holmes had dropped it on the floor. A small card slipped out of the folds and floated to the carpet. It too was of excellent quality paper with a superior block printed name, address, and title. Watson read it; then read it again. The name seemed to call someone to mind, though he couldn't place it.

"What is it, Watson?"

"More data."

.

Late November 1883
The Swans Saloon on Sacramento Street
The Barbary Coast, San Francisco, California

To call the establishment and its denizens "derelict" would perhaps serve as a compliment. Throughout the Barbary Coast, surviving within its imprisonment between Stockton Street and Montgomery Avenue – California Street and Broadway, there were finer watering holes and gambling dens. Most were located as far away from Pacific Street, on the northern end of the neighborhood, as they could get. The Swans was indeed closer to the better part of San Francisco, but the location had not served to improve things.

Turner leaned against the bar and smiled at the woman setting up a glass for him. She was the perfect distraction. Blonde, big eyed, and plush in her figure. She knew what she was doing. She was also quite likely ten years younger than she looked and as the saying went, was "rode hard, put away wet." She wasn't beautiful anymore, though she might have been once. Now, she was living on her wits and she had vulgar street knowledge in her arsenal.

So did he. He knew he was nothing to look at yet, wearing second hand clothing, sporting a scrappy, untrimmed beard, smudged dirt on his hands and face, and that filthy fisherman's cap. A dark blue bandana served as both a neck tie, for no man of any rank stepped out into public without neckwear of some sort, and a means to cover the hanging scar – something that would make him too memorable. He was virtually invisible against a backdrop of lowlifes, jay-hawkers, thieves and bummers. The woman behind the bar had no reason to want his particular attention since he appeared to have limited funds – which he did. If she worked on her back, in one of the brick-oven rooms, he was not the sort she'd gravitate to. Men who looked like Turner promised gold and delivered tin. Experience alone would teach her not to ply a trade with little guarantee the client would pay. No, her role was not to sell herself; she was the distraction in this game.

She kept her lips tight in a grin, so as not to show that she had bad teeth, poured his drink, and rested her hands on the opposite side of the bar. She held her arms close together to prop up her weight and to press her breasts together, lifting and accentuating her cleavage for Turner's approval. She wasn't the type to come through with her promises either. That was not her job anymore. "Need anything else?"

He calmly played with the drink but didn't raise the glass. The movement of his hands kept her eyes on them and not the face he hid in the shadow of his cap. Drinks were often laced with opium or something uglier. That or this was likely bad whisky as such an establishment didn't have anything of quality. "A good *smithy*," he replied, using that well-worn euphemism for a dealer in stolen guns. A blue haze of opium smoke and flavored tobacco drifted out of the nostrils of men, clung to the ceiling and wafted down to the crowded Faro tables like the fog outside. The floor was dirty and sticky from God only knew what liquids were spilled on it. Ah, there it is, he noted, the seam between the floor and the hatch which had opened under a number of hopeless men's feet. Good men never seen again. Turner shifted his stance and moved one foot off the trap. Such places had earned their nickname, "deadfalls," all too well. "Got to be a fella' around here who handles ... *repairs*."

She giggled a little, at nothing in particular. "Yeah, we got those here. Real good with repairs."

Indeed! That was a sure sign she was a distraction; she gave away useful information she could have normally bartered for. In a Barbary Coast saloon, a sailor had to be alert.

"Two blocks down – past China alley - gray building – entrance in the back. He's got a nice shop full of ... repairs."

But of course she would tell him that. Either the shop was legitimate and she would want the gun dealer to know he owed *her* for a customer reference, or that was another place one of the "Crimps" was going to try to shanghai Turner. He was betting on the latter.

He still smiled back. Coming on to him was her job and she was absolutely responsible for the kidnapping of sailors, but there was no need to be rude. "Thank you, Miss."

Turner's hand slipped out of his pocket, knife out of its sheath, and settled it above the kidney of the man who had come within reach behind him. The man stopped and his eyes became huge. The woman behind the counter was surprised too.

Slowly, Turner set down the glass, none of its contents consumed, and turned around to the man who had tried to sneak up on him. "Tell me you aren't looking for blood money off these poor old bones of mine?" Shanghaiing agents were paid in what survivors called blood money, an all too apt description. The Crimp looked to be about Turner's age yet physically worn out from the kidnapping business and prematurely aged from the viciousness of survival. His face was pock-marked, eyes sunken, and a large belly from rotten food distended outward. "Let me explain it to you: I've been to sea, thank you. Don't plan to go back, certainly not on your ticket. Just spent the last months getting home from the Indies and I'm all done with travel. You do understand me, yes? Just nod. Good. Then let me make myself clearer still. You and I are going to see a dealer. If there's no dealer, I'll cut your kidney out and serve it to this little lady. She said two blocks down. Now ... no, no, don't try to get away from me ... two blocks down. What's there ... really?"

"I don't know what ..." his voice suddenly squealed. Turner's knife pushed harder and slightly lower. "Alright! You ... ah ... you don't want to go there."

"That's very considerate of you to tell me. Where should a man like me, in need of repairs, go? Excuse me Miss, but please don't move from where you are. You look quite lovely just standing there."

The blonde woman froze in place against the bar.

The Crimp was sweating. It took virtually none of his imagination to realize that he would not receive assistance in time before the sailor he'd mistaken for an easy mark would slice him in half. The woman wasn't moving and none of his colleagues had registered the notion that something was wrong. By all appearances, he and his intended victim were having a gentlemanly chat.

Turner hated to say it, but his survival depended on his skill with threats. "Now Miss, my new friend and I are going to take a little stroll. You should just stay put. I know exactly who you are and where you are if you send his friends after us. I would be very unhappy if I needed to deal with you in an impolite manner. I'd prefer by far to remember you and your gracious visage, just as you are." God in Heaven that tasted bad to say. He'd never been comfortable threatening women, not even the worst of them.

"Girl, get Bolger and the other boys. This bastard ain't

19

enough to take all of us." The Crimp tried to sound tough, but failed miserably. "Are you mister?" His voice squeaked a little.

"Go to hell!" she spit. "I ain't getting ripped up for you. You owe me from the last one. And you ain't half as polite as him or look half as good."

Turner leaned in toward the Crimp, which was not pleasant in any terms as the man had not bathed in a considerable amount of time. "I also know you and can easily find you ... by smell if nothing else. I'll find out if she has any trouble over this, and I'll send her something of your corpse in the mail." The knife lowered and prodded a couple of times. "Shall we take a walk?"

The Crimp nodded emphatically.

Outside the Swans, no one really cared if Turner was keeping the Crimp at knife point though he did put some effort into making things appear congenial. Most of the thick crowd kept their heads down and avoided eye contact at all costs. Chinese porters or "coolies," carrying outrageous burdens on bamboo poles, maneuvered through the throng of drunks with remarkable grace. Horses left their droppings behind to be worn down with age until they faded into the dirt. The smell remained. A fight broke out on the other side of the Swans. Several women sashayed along the walkway, nodding and winking at potential customers. The worst of humanity had managed to huddle together in a fraction of the city, doing whatever injury they could to each other and themselves. From the dance cellars, a cacophony of noise rose above the filthy street; a clash of laughter, angry shouts, curses, and colliding musical instruments. The discord added a surreal tint to the slightly dreamy state Turner noticed he was shaking off. The opium laced smoke had affected him more than he'd anticipated. The Crimp was a half step ahead of him and couldn't see him fighting off the drug-encouraged stupor. Cold air, filtered through the dense, incoming fog, helped keep him awake and on guard.

He'd have to deal harshly with the Crimp – and soon – as he couldn't trust how much the opium smoke would slow him down. A giggle from a threesome of girls caught his attention. They were South American, he thought. Beautiful, young, and probably too expensive for most of the men around them, thus the giggling. Behind them an older Chinese woman in blue silk satin, black loose trousers, and white soled embroidered shoes, carried a basket of goods on her back. She was probably a merchant's wife and no longer bothered by any of the disgusting behavior around her. There was every possibility that she was one of the girls who had escaped prostitution through marriage, though it was unlikely – she would not want to be near this world if she'd run away from it.

All this and it wasn't nighttime yet. The Barbary Coast would get worse the darker the day grew. And … the closer to Pacific Street they got.

The drug-induced daze seemed to be wearing off as they approached China Alley. Turner took only a moment to look. The windows were filled with painted faces of working girls – slaves really. They were sold off by their families in China, brought to the "land of the free" and sold into misery. The chances of breaking away from this hell were none. Before the sound of a slamming door jarred him away from his thoughts, he sadly wondered how many would create their own, final, way out? Or how many would merely "disappear" once they were no longer young and lovely – and marketable.

The crack of wood on wood reminded him for a second of the trap falling out from under his feet – at Andersonville Prison – slamming into the scaffold. His throat constricted and swallowing was labored. Such a reaction was so common to him; it never lasted long.

Turner pressed his knife harder into the Crimp's back near his kidneys. Threat re-established: just in case the Crimp was feeling that same hazy, opium state. Ahead, an alley waited where the gun dealer's place of business was supposed to be. A dead end alley waited, shadowed even in fading daylight. The barwoman had given him false instructions. She was a very lucky gal: if he had been the killer he'd let her think he was, she would be in dreadful danger. But Turner had no intention of following through with his well placed warning.

The Crimp, on the other hand, did not deserve any special forgiveness or consideration. As though expecting Turner to be furious at the lie, the Crimp stopped. With heavy breaths, and more profuse sweating, he turned his head slightly back. "This ain't it. She done you a big disservice, mister. That's Sally. Blame her. Me? I'll git you to the right place. No lies; no tricks. You lookin' for somethin' special?"

"Not that you need to know about."

"Suit yerself. Ain't that interested in you. Cept, I hope to read about you in the papers, 'cause someone'll take ill to your ways."

Turner smiled and said, rather sarcastically, "I'm stunned."

"Why? 'Cause I wanna see you dead?"

"No. You can read."

Behind the gun shop, the *actual* gun seller's shop located in a basement not otherwise occupied by gamblers or Chinese dice players, the Crimp woke up with the worst headache he'd ever known, and was lucky to be alive based on the near-crippling blow he'd received to the back of his skull. He hadn't been unconscious for but a moment. A bunch of whores had found him there and laughed at him.

He staggered back to his usual saloon, far from the one where he'd tangled with the stranger. Damp clung to everything, and wisps of fog shrouded the few gas lamps in the area, thick enough to hide signs of civilization.

From the dark void of un-illuminated fog that covered the bay beyond the city limits came a droning whine, low and quick to fade like a howling dog. Then the thumping: steady, rhythmic, dangerous. Such eerie noises had been spoken of in soft conversations but rarely out loud. If the Crimp had learned nothing else, he had learned that it was a bad idea to learn too much and to speak of it aloud. Like seemingly everyone else, he chose to ignore it as none of his business. Besides, he had more pressing issues.

The smithy said the stranger was now packing two *custom-made* Colts, originally made for someone else and very unwillingly parted with, along with several boxes of ammunition. Easy trigger. Easily reloaded.

Wonderful. Now he could get shot too. Knifed then shot, or was it shot then knifed? No, this mark was getting away and good riddance. Maybe it was a good thing Sally hadn't told Bolger or any of the boys about what happened. He could pretend it was nothing and forget it all soon enough.

But, his friends who waited for him knew something they weren't telling him. Shouting did little good, until someone mentioned that they knew who the stranger was. Hadn't he seen the scar? Someone else had been looking for the man. Somebody far scarier than the Crimp or Bolger. Good, the Crimp thought, drowning his pain in booze. I hope they kill him, he thought. And yeah, I can *read* about it. Sorta. He reached into his pocket to throw a coin at the bartender for his drink and froze. His pocket was empty. All his pockets were empty. Oh hell!

Late November 1883
The Palace Hotel on Montgomery Street
San Francisco, California

By the late afternoon of the next day, Tom Turner had done what he was becoming masterful at doing: he changed into something so radically different in appearance that there would be no recognizing what had been before.

Seemed the Crimp had won a bit at gambling earlier and had not hidden it away properly or wisely. Coins, paper bills and wage chips had been carelessly shoved into his pockets. His biggest error, beyond taking on Turner in the first place, was choosing to go have a drink at the Swans before securing his money. What a shame. Taking the Crimp's money wasn't ethical but somehow it seemed fitting. The money was now properly placed in *his* boot until he could find a much more secure place for it. His *new* boots. Two hundred and fifty dollars. Where the man had managed to win over two hundred dollars was a mystery Turner had absolutely no intention of bothering to solve. At least it wasn't Blood Money. That would never have stayed in any Crimp's pocket, not even one as stupid as the one he'd pistol whipped. It was worth a Crimp's life should he lose or mishandle it. Blood Money went to the crime lords who would never forgive lost profits. Two hundred and fifty dollars was not so much to lose for the syndicates that ran the shanghai business, but it was too much to be forgiven. Besides, Blood Money came only in paper form: it was easier to handle, lighter, and spent as well as coinage. It could even be deposited legitimately in one of the numerous banks in the city. The ship captains who purchased shanghaied sailors knew to keep things business-like and wouldn't send payments in chips and assorted cash.

He could never have brought himself to take Blood Money and spend it on clothing and luxury.

In his respectable new suit, bathed, clipped and trimmed, cheroots inside his coat, and sporting a simple but fashionable hat,

Turner was a new man. And he had now two disguises to move about in. The given clothes would serve him well if he needed to play down his existence, and right now he needed to appear as gentlemanly as possible to hide among the wealthy. No one would recognize that the fellow sipping coffee and prodding at an oyster or two was indeed the same scruffy fellow who had rented a room in the seedier side of the town. Generally unrecognizable from his previous state, he could move around without worrying over curious police, angry crimps, or Hetzel's killers.

He kept the goatee and moustache since it was distinct from his prior appearances and would wear the hat low on his forehead to alter the perception of his head's shape. If needed, he could let a day's growth return to his cheeks and again his appearance would alter. He had been tempted toward tinted glasses but decided it was incongruous with proper attire and might even draw more attention to him.

Tempting too was the notion of moving into a beautiful suite at the Palace. He knew better. The money would only go so far and he was better off saving it. The oysters, however, were a bit of an indulgence. Inside the valise at his side were his "unfashionables." He would easily don those again to go back to his affordable accommodations.

Turner watched the room, taking note of the afternoon patrons, many of whom were of a class of people who had afternoons free to dine. Before he could stop himself, he'd noted how many of the fashionable gowns the ladies were wearing would look infinitely better on Lettie Gantry.

As at home as she would have been on the edge of the Hawai'ian volcano, she would be at ease in such surroundings as the Tea Room. The Palace glittered with chandeliers, crystal and gold leaf. The Persian carpets were in delightfully vulgar shades of red, orange, and blue. Each table was inlaid with various exotic woods in intricate patterns. And the service was quite good. All very tony. All very expected of those who called San Francisco the *Venice of the West*. Oh yes, Lettie would be very happy here - until someone was appalled by her vocation as a scientist or acted dismissively toward her intelligence because she was a woman.

In the corner, somewhat away from the main body of diners, was a table often reserved for gentlemen. He could guess that much as the settings were elegant but uncluttered with feminine touches. A whisky cart was stationed near it which either meant the table was commonly used by gentlemen or the ladies of San Francisco were more liberal than noted by the outside world.

Sure enough, the men began to file in. Dressed to be seen, they were as bad as any of the women and probably worse in their gossip. It was man who generally held more contempt for someone who had wronged him but the woman who was burdened with the reputation. And, in fairness, Turner had had his own such moments. One of the men had a strong, Southern drawl, and it grated on Turner's ears. He closed his eyes for a moment and pushed aside any memories from the war. It was long over. Two decades since. He had to be more forgiving, and expecting a fight with Southerners who were no threat to him was a waste of his energy. He had to save it all for Hetzel's next move. He needed to be ready.

A waiter approached with more coffee, poured from an exquisite pot of polished silver. He offered Turner a tray on which waited the largest local newspaper. Ah, such a luxury. It would be essential for him to understand the politics and any strange activities of the city he was in. Yet, to sit and enjoy the aroma of roasted coffee beans, fresh oysters, and the tactile feel of a newspaper in his hands … it was perhaps a momentary heaven. And, worth the relatively small expense.

One headline announced details of King David Kalākaua's coronation, something Turner wished he could have stayed in Hawai'i to see. The journalist was at minimum polite in his description of the newly crowned King, but not really very accurate.

Several honest citizens had written letters to the editor to complain of late night – pre-dawn sounds coming from the industrial areas and more so to complain about the lack of response to their demands from the Mayor. They were, after all, *honest* citizens. Horrible groaning; thumping; roaring – all sounds one expects from angry ghosts, though for his part, Turner knew a thing or two on that subject. Turner read one of the letters a second time, and smiled, thinking how San Francisco was at any moment on the verge of being a ghost town should the gold run out. Perhaps the ghosts weren't willing to wait on the living.

Over half of the paper was filled with advertisements. Horses were for rent everywhere. Especially near the toll road to Point

Lobos and the Cliff House. Horses? Turner grinned and hoped no one noticed. He was such a poor horseman, as he had discovered near Kilauea.

Now, here was some news. He'd suspected it for some time but hadn't had enough current information to verify any of his concerns. Prussia and Great Britain were rattling sabers at one another. That was a fairly standard, almost comical annual event. For his own part, Turner could recall too well learning of how the Prussians intervened in the Civil War, of how they provided hundreds of spy balloons to Richmond, of how they shared improvements to cannons and mortars ... of how Union soldiers occasionally came up against skilled, disciplined Prussian officers. Never with a pleasant ending.

Of course, rumors abounded that the Prussians brought more than fancy cannons, professional soldiers, and big hot air balloons. Stories echoed from the halls of Congress to the campsites on the Mississippi; strange metal creatures and machines, rumbling through the hills near Shiloh and Vicksburg.

Turner folded the international portion of the paper back with a snap. Those rumors had nothing on what he'd seen since the war ended. Nothing like the machine he faced in Hawai'i. And all of them designed with the sole intention of killing men for power and greed. It made no sense to him.

So, when the South lost, Prussia took the failure with dignity and turned its fury on France. Spain gave up the last of her territories in the Americas and began guarding its only remaining colony in the Philippine Islands.

So, Prussia was back to attempting territorial gains and power brokering. Some things never changed.

The gentlemen at the fine table suddenly ceased chatting.

Turner held up the newspaper and leaned back, as though he was too important to notice such a sudden silence and the feeling he was being stared at.

New naval personnel had arrived to take up offices near Hunter's Point. He knew a few names vaguely. One stood out: Benjamin Thomas Willey. An old friend. He likely couldn't just drop by and say hello: he was disgraced, at least in his own mind, from his escapades with Robur the Conqueror. No honest man who knew of his past, would want the connection. Too bad. He liked Willey who

27

was a good man with a smart head on his shoulders. He would have liked a long talk over bourbon and cigars.

As he turned the page, a crackle of paper following the motion, he narrowed his attention toward the table. Taking the paper in one hand, he allowed himself a slow reach for his coffee, and over the rim of the cup, he glanced at the gathering of men. One stared at him; the others tried not looking.

Turner knew they couldn't see his scar. Current fashion demanded a high, starched collar that prodded the underside of the jaw. Over that was wrapped a splendid silk tie of such a color that it tricked the eye into believing that the discolored skin was merely a reflection the fabric's tint. So, what were they staring at?

A hiss from the coffee machine, with its twisting pipe for delivering steaming hot water from the cookers to the expressing presses, made Turner grip the paper more tightly but he refused to allow more reaction than that.

He folded the paper, leaving the latest advertisements for the American Pneumatic Transmission and Communication Company and the Reuters News and Heavy Transport Service staring up at the ceiling, along with those for standard glycerin soap, healthful corsetry, and pre-starched collars.

The interested gentleman had descended the pair of carpeted steps near his table and had arrived at Turner's table. "Good afta'noon, sir." The drawl was thicker than Turner had originally heard. Georgia? Carolinas? He could feel his muscles tensing automatically. "I hope you will forgive my intrusion. My companions and I are businessmen, working for the betterment of this fine city. We are always on the lookout for gentlemen of similar philosophy with which to form new acquaintances."

Move slowly, Turner reminded himself. Gentlemen of leisure are never hurried. He pushed his paper forward on the table and gracefully rose to take measure of the man who was intruding on his midday meal. The fellow was close to Turner's height, broad in the shoulder and belly, and Turner was certain that he was carrying some sort of firearm on his side based on the way he held his arm. Turner stepped back so that the man couldn't closely scrutinize his face or throat. Before his slow pace insinuated an insult by suggesting the lack of importance of the man, Turner offered his hand. "How do you do, sir." He mimicked Lettie's accent.

"Splendid. And I hope y'all are enjoying our fair city thus far?"

"Indeed, sir, indeed. It would be difficult not to."

"Do I detect a slight English edge to your speech, sir?"

He smiled to the man who was expecting him to be a dandy, or a foreign "greenhorn" who was ill suited to the wild life in the far western towns. It was time to put him off. The last thing Turner wanted was the attention of a man old enough to have been a plantation owner or Confederate soldier. It wasn't fair of him to snap to that judgment but if he could dislodge himself from further discourse it would make him considerably happier. "Yes, sir, I am a British subject by birth. I have, I daresay, been abroad for some years, though I am entirely familiar with the west." You may feel free to interpret that, Turner thought, as an indicator that I am a man of the world and not at all green. "As you say, sir, this is a fair city and I feel quite at home here."

"I hope that y'all are not offended at my assumption that y'all are new?"

"Not in the least sir. I am entirely satisfied to have made your acquaintance."

The smile that was produced for Turner's appreciation was forced. The man was hiding any number of thoughts, or so his body language showed, but in his conversation he offered as much charm as he could muster. "Perhaps we shall have an opportunity to meet again?"

Turner rarely liked the outcome when people sought opportunities to "meet again." It was never based on the knowledge that the soon-to-be meeting would be auspicious – the reasons varying from circumstance to circumstance. From experience, he knew that the man had already decided where and when the next meeting would occur. "That would be delightful. As I am a guest," he said, declining to state exactly where he was a guest, "I would like to think we'll run into one another here sometime soon."

"Yes. Indeed, sir. Indeed."

The gentlemen had left their table one at a time after Turner had made all the proper motions of paying his bill and heading toward the elevators. Interesting, he thought, how the man who spoke to him managed to avoid providing his name or a place to contact him. No card was provided, which was probably just as well as Turner did not have a gentleman's or a businessman's card as of yet. Such an absence would have given rise to uncomfortable questions. Any man of means had a card. For a moment, Turner considered if he had the funds to order a set, but then, what name would he use? What profession?

At the front desk, he made a point of asking about the safety of the elevator system from the Bell Captain, who was quite amazed when Turner knew more about the engineering of such contraptions than the average guest. It wasn't that the elevator was new, it had been around since the 50's, but they were quickly becoming as efficient as they were ornate. The whole frontage of the San Francisco business district and wharfs was packed with the marvels, run by hydraulic steam or high pressure water mains that were established all along the waterfront.

It was ultimately not an important subject to Turner, he simply wanted to provide information to one of the gentlemen who had remained behind to spy on him. Now they, whoever *they* were, if they were anyone worth worrying over or not, would know that he was intelligent, possibly a businessman working with mechanicals, and most importantly: they would assume he was staying at the hotel — why else bother about the elevators at all?

The poor fellow tasked with following Turner abandoned his duty on the lazy assumption that Turner was on his way to his room. Instead, he carelessly allowed Turner to follow him. The fellow stopped for a drink and a chat with a well dressed merchant, giving Turner time to swap out clothing. He never noticed the scrappy bum who kept a few yards behind him.

Down Market Street, then east toward the bay. Turner knew he wouldn't be able to get into the building the fellow staggered into, without looking out of place. Still, he had a vaguely sick feeling as he looked at the enormous warehouse. In letters larger than him, the five story building declared the facility to be the *Asian Pacific and Southern Airship, Railroad, and Overland Wagon Company.* The letters were bounded by a line drawing of a large dirigible balloon. It was a gentle looking thing, with no sharp lines or dynamic placement to make the advertisement appear aggressive.

It set Turner's teeth on edge.

He would need to come back here.

Late November 1883
The Asian Pacific and Southern Airship, Railroad, and
Overland Wagon Company, San Francisco, California

A night later, Turner put his offensive plan into play.

San Francisco was draping itself with a blanket of fog, to hunker down for the night – though perhaps not over in the Barbary Coast. Deep fog horns bellowing out a hollow, haunted tone from deep in the bowels of numerous lighthouses only wreaked havoc on the imagination. Perhaps those good citizens who'd written to the papers to complain of horrible noises in the night had mistaken the mismatched fog horns, though that seemed unlikely. The low ceiling created by the City's famous weather accomplished the task of keeping surface temperatures warmer, hiding what shouldn't be seen, and causing every step to have a tremendous echo where one might have supposed it would have dampened any sound. Clanging bells and docksides being bumped by ocean-going vessels sounded as close as a stone's throw, but in reality were about three quarters of a mile away.

The fog also provided illusions for the nose as well as the eyes. The smells of wood soaked in sea brine and rusting iron floated all the way up the slope, to be matched by industrial stench.

Stranger things hid in the protected corners and damp shadows.

While secrets of the latest improvements to road, rail and air-cargo transportation were generally well guarded, the number of locks, bolts and chains Turner had to work through to get into the offices were outrageous in number. It was not that Turner couldn't pick a lock or disable a simple trap, it was the time it took to accomplish his task. Several times he stopped to listen for the sounds of dogs he was sure he had heard. But no. God in Heaven, couldn't they have just left a window open for him to crawl through.

The office of the Asian Pacific and Southern company was as typical as any cargo company's interior. The president of the company had an office with as much opulence as was possible. Lush appointments included an enormous walnut desk with gold plated pens, ink wells, and blotters. Books that had little to no wear to them suggested that they were purchased for show rather than for the use of the man who kept the office. A cloying scent of old cigars and cigarettes lingered on the walls and sofa. Deep burgundy velvet curtains were drawn shut.

Outside were several less luxurious offices, though they provided a suggestion of prosperity required by middle level managers. Less gold and fewer lavish items. Such offices were instead filled with popular clutter and hemmed in by garish paintings of country scenes. Strangely, one manager had several such paintings of plantations.

The clerk's offices were small, sparse, and cold. Typical.

Beyond another bolted door lay the warehouse that was the key to the mystery. After listening for several minutes, Turner opened the door minimally, ready for creaking or squealing, and crept into the gigantic room. It was at least twenty times larger than the section of the building housing the offices. It was set into a deep, excavated hole in the side of the hill and the offices led straight out onto a platform suspended above. Tracks of standard gauge ran the length of the manufacturing area — yet there were no locomotives. Another platform at the top of a flight of stairs part way to the roof, would have been perfect for a suspended lead airship gondola or a set of dirigibles used for heavy goods transportation — yet no airship filled the space. The warehouse itself was not on the bay, thus there was hardly any chance one would see ship to shore unloading. No wagons, no sign of mules, and in fact, nothing.

He stole slowly down the metal stairs, listening for any signal that there were others here. Near the bottom, he could smell the odors of heated metal, grease, and decay. In the dimmed light, he could see nothing that appeared to be a completed design. So how, he wondered silently, does a transport company stay in business without transport? Did they have only a few wagons or a single dirigible? They'd been in business since 1872, so there really was no excuse for them not to have expanded their operations and purchased additional, necessary equipment.

Turner held his tiny phosphorus lantern up as high as he could. In Hawai'i, he'd obtained the little object, proud that he had been able to use it then, and now to have kept it. It produced an odd, orange glow.

What he could see were crates of rivets, unused, stacked near the tracks. Turner stooped next to the wooden box filled only a quarter with the iron bits. There had been many more here. Had they been used on something substantial? Shavings of iron lay all over the floor. Cut metal sheets and welding material waited in the shadows.

A nail dropped onto the airship platform and bounced several steps down before stopping.

Turner held his breath. Who was there? The Colt revolver, sitting in a back holster, seemed to press into his spine. Never draw a weapon unless you are going to use it right then, or need someone to know you have it, he reminded himself. If he was being watched, he needed to keep his gun hidden until the last second. Hastily drawn and thoughtlessly pointed guns usually meant someone was getting shot – often the shooter.

He extinguished the light and waited.

Wind pushed through broken windows near the ceiling and produced an odd whistling sound.

A door rattled. The bay breeze was picking up.

He let his breath out.

Cold air was coming from the wall too. Perhaps there was an opening, but he doubted it. The building was a fortress in most ways. A careless opening could invite anyone, even a former sailor, to break in.

There was a rumbling. Low and heavy. It had a rhythm, steady, slow, shaking the ground. It was not an earthquake. It was too small, too perfect, too long in duration.

Outside of the big loading doors, lights burst through the cracks. Bright lights. A long, screeching hiss echoed around the empty warehouse. The biggest door rattled again, forcefully.

That was not the wind.

Backing into a corner, he prayed could hide in the shadows. Turner crouched down and waited, partially shielded by a heavy metal plate. Voices and the puffing, huffing, regular thumping sound of pistons being driven by force, back and forth. The great hiss sprayed burning fog under the door and shrouded the outside from view as the doors opened.

Several shouts preceded the *iron dragon*. Where natives had called the original locomotives the "iron horse," this was nothing shy of a beast of legend. Only a handful of men were on the ground to escort it into the warehouse. It was gigantic, but somehow that didn't surprise Turner. This was an age when everyone tried to outdo one another; if not through shocking cleverness then through outrageous size. This beast was exactly that. It rumbled and quaked the floor of the warehouse with its weight.

The locomotive was not elegant, but had its own odd beauty. It moved quietly – without squealing or rattling against the tracks, which took some sort of fresh, innovative design as four hundred tons never otherwise moved without sound. The floor groaned under the weight. Only the thump, thump, thump of the pistons – and it shook him through his chest with each pounding. Then the explosion of scalding water vapor escaping its confines produced a terrifying roar.

Its wheels were the size of a man, with window-paned cores. For once, someone had figured out how to make a train's wheel lighter by eliminating any unnecessary metal. That was the most obvious innovation, but hardly the only one. Turner dared to lean forward only a fraction to watch as it was positioned completely inside the warehouse.

Light from the locomotive cab had that same, odd orange color to it. The designer had incorporated similar chemistry as had been used in Turner's lantern. Once the warehouse doors were closed, he understood that this engine was not coupled to cars or a coal bunker; just the engine which was clearly being tried and tested.

Realizing he was at ground level and that any steam from the boiler would likely blast out again under high pressure, he looked around urgently for a place where he was less likely to be scalded to death. One of them signaled and the crew swiftly backed far away from the engine.

The locomotive hissed then emptied her belly of every ounce of built up vapor. It shot out from the undercarriage and the steam dome, almost erasing it from sight in a bank of white cloud. Everything immediately around it was boiled or scrubbed clean by the force.

Turner pulled his leg though the hole in the wall just in the nick of time. The temperature around him plunged. He had crawled under the building, into the foundation. The hole between the foundation and the warehouse was from neglect, or so it appeared.

The metal plates had hidden it from easy view of those who worked in the building.

He had an alternate place to hide. He crept back to the opening in the wall to watch, once he was sure the engine had vented all of its excess steam.

The body of the locomotive was longer by two thirds than a regular rail engine. Taller by the same, but if it used the standard track gage, it was not wider. It appeared encased and angular. The pistons appeared to be single cast steel bars which had been blackened in a dull, non-reflective paint. So too the reach rod, throttles, pumps, foot boards. Why blackened, he wondered? To keep them from shining in sun or moonlight? Would that help keep this monstrosity hidden? Why try to hide it?

The shape of the beast appeared about the same as the average locomotive, but had the look of something made in the same manner as the pistons: cast steel – all of it blackened. The short, straight stack was made from several layers of iron, riveted into a column, and sealed with gum – perfect for coal burning engines: funnel shaped stakes denoted wood burners. Yet, there was the curious thing: a smoke stack with no smoke. He hadn't a clear view but what he could see suggested the stack was sealed off. Impossible. The smoke from the burnt fuel had to go somewhere. Only Robur, his late commander, had created an engine that emitted no smoke. Turner was desperate to get closer.

Turner waited while a man in overalls and a dark cap inspected the grease levels nearest the drive shafts. Satisfied, he leaned a huge grease gun against the side of the engine.

Pipes dripped with water but the steam pressure had dropped considerably. It was safer for him to get close, in relative terms. Turner slowly climbed back through the hole and waited in the shadows for his chance. Ears straining for the slightest sound: a voice, a foot step, a buildup of pressure.

The cab was laid out in the typical manner, with a seat for the engineer on the right and a seat for the fireman on the left. Central was the boiler and its heat source. The door between the offices and the warehouse opened and closed. The man in the overalls had gone up there. A moment later, voices of men closing the big doors and discussing something indeterminate followed the first fellow upstairs. Lights in the clerk's office came up as each gas lamp was illuminated.

Turner crept closer to the cab, until he was standing, touching the bottom rung of the ladder. His left hand rested on the ladder rail, his right on the grip of his Colt at his back – finger close to the trigger.

The boiler caught his eye first. Wires, wrapped together in bundles, were inserted through holes created in the boiler cover. There was no sign of coal or wood or any other combustible to heat the water – hence, no smoke.

He stepped up one rung of the iron, Swiss-holed steps. Listening. Slowly breathing. Hands sweating.

He was a sailor not a soldier. His experience had been with boats and sailing vessels, and later with Robur's airship. The army used the railroad to superb effect during the war. Yet, as a sailor, he knew no more about locomotives than an average school boy might. There were things he knew were standard and those that weren't. The boiler should have had a great fire burning inside the firebox on the grate, with coal as its main fuel. That would have left thick, black dust on everything and a smell that was distinctive. He saw none.

The wires suggested one thing: electricity. So the Asian Pacific and Southern railroad was electrified: they had discovered what Robur had known regarding electric engines of substantial power. There were likely two or more Wimshurst generators inside. Robur had used the same process for the *Albatross* and Nemo, his *Nautilus*. The French were working on something close, with some success in their passenger service. Now it appeared that an American company was quickly catching up. But how did they start the generators and maintain any surplus supply of electric charge unless they had a very basic fuel-fired boiler system? This had been Robur's challenge and why Lettie Gantry had been abducted: she could help naturally occurring lightning in volcanic eruption clouds – Robur's bizarre, risky, yet moderately successful jump-starter for his engines. The Asian Pacific and Southern was certainly not chasing down potential volcanic eruptions, so what was their source of fuel for the initial start up of the generators? What did they do with the excess electricity?

He climbed the second rung and looked into the slightly ajar boiler door – they were allowing it to cool slowly. Long tubes with water were arranged every other one, parallel with tubes holding the wires. Like the *Albatross*, the wires were electrically heated and boiled the water. The steam, when the boiler was in operation, would collect centrally and pressure would build. Resulting steam was shunted either into the Wimshurst generators or out to the main pipe and into the cylinders. The Wimshurst generators would energize the heating wires and so the process repeated. Those generators were not small. Excess steam was collected and returned to the water compartment to be used again. Other than the electrically generated heat for the boilers, the locomotive appeared normal – simply larger.

Finally, he could see the fuel burner hidden deeper into the body of the locomotive. It was better protected. And it appeared to use a liquid fuel, not coal, hence the lack of stench and dust. Well done, he thought. He recognized its value in a land-based vessel. Coal or liquid, it was heavy and if he had learned anything from Robur, it was that "airship" and "heavy" should never be terms used mutually to describe the same flying craft.

So, what was the liquid made of? Turner started up toward the top rung.

The office door banged open with a heated discussion floating out into the warehouse.

Turner backed down the ladder, spun around to flee back into his shadows, and found the lubricating tool with his shin. The huge metal instrument, which looked more like a grotesque hypodermic needle with grease oozing out of it, clattered loudly as it hit the ground.

The discussion stopped. "Someone's down there!"

Turner dashed to the wall and then to his hole. His trouser was torn at the shin and he imagined he had a good cut deep in the skin. He had no time to stop and check.

Behind him, he could hear more voices and one solid, scrapping pump of a shotgun.

He stopped and pressed his back against the foundation bricks, his hand on the pistol, hesitating. He was the intruder. They could shoot him if they wanted to for trespassing or spying. If he shot back, the law would not be favorable to him. But if he had to …

"The greaser fell over." The man in the overalls sounded annoyed.

"It was knocked over. Those things don't move on their own."

Turner could feel a slight breeze and decided that there must be a way through the building's foundation floor. They hadn't found the hole yet. He had time. Not much, but he had it. He couldn't see a damn thing, not even his feet.

The dirt was not solidly packed. He tore away a face full of spider webs. Each step he took, he made sure there was ground to step on and no more objects that would signal his whereabouts.

"Hey, there's something here!"

"If it was someone nosing around, find him!"

He stretched his hand out to feel for the breeze. It was coming from a point not far ahead. Light. Not much, but enough. Voices behind him. His leg was throbbing. Light, from under a door or a blacked-out window? His hands struck on a wooden door. An old coal door. There had to be a handle. Was it locked?

The door didn't challenge him in the least. An old coal storage no longer used, leading only to the foundation … who cared if it was unlocked. The hole in the wall? Had someone made that to spy on the locomotive builders? Oh hell, did it even matter. If someone had made that hole, they'd left the door unlocked. Wait — how long ago had that person been there?

"What's down there?"

"Foundation. Ain't no way out. Maybe there wasn't someone?"

"Don't take no chances. Search it!"

Taking a deep breath, knowing that the opened door would flood the area with light and give him away, Turner pushed hard on it and ran.

"Someone's here! Someone's here!"

A shot rang out, but had to have gone wild. Nothing ricocheted near him. Two more shots. One came close. But only two more shots. He let go the grip on his pistol and left it snug in the holster. This was not the time or place for a fire fight. Turner stayed his course and ran as hard as his legs would carry him. He changed direction twice. Dodged down short alleys. Finally, he found himself back on Market Street.

Peals of laughter from bordellos and watering holes greeted him along with a flood of fog dampened street lamps.

Dressed in his poor man's togs he immediately blended in. Snatching the cap from his head and shoving it into his coat pocket, then wrapping his coat around his waist, he changed his silhouette and Turner slowed his pace. He stuck his hands in his pockets and began to stagger as though drunk.

Had he lost the men chasing him?

He came up to a building that housed a saloon and music hall. As he leaned near the front window, a man ran full speed up behind him.

The man looked at each of the drunks and bums outside. The bulge in his coat pocket was clearly caused by his right hand and a gun.

He stared at Turner.

Turner glared back at him with a lack of sobriety and started to say, in vulgar slurred pronunciation, "ya wan' som-tin? Blow uff, Jack! I ... I ... gots no biss-ness wid' ju." He took two drunken steps toward the armed man.

He stared at Turner with disgust this time, spit, and walked away. Two more men ran up to him and they in turn continued their search down the street.

Carefully, drunkenly, he leaned himself against a gas lamp and took a look at his shin. It was cut, but not as deeply as he thought. Blood had already hardened and an ugly bruise formed around the wound. It could well have been worse. He slumped against the lamp pole until he was sitting, pulled out a kerchief and covered up the cut. No point in begging further damage or infection.

There were about seven men playing cards on the walkway three yards down. With 75 cents, Turner joined the game and played well enough until he lost all of it somewhere around sun up. It was worth the loss. Every ten minutes or so, the men from the Asian Pacific and Southern searched the crowds on the street. It wouldn't be safe for him to leave. By sunrise, they had given up and were headed back to the warehouse.

The denizens of the Market Street evening began to shuffle home; Turner with them. Make no attempt to rush or run, he reminded himself.

That day, he slept fitfully and hungry, certain at any moment those men would show up at his shabby hotel room demanding answers.

He was too exhausted to think clearly. He wanted to know why the gentlemen at the Palace Hotel were so interested in him and what was it they were building in the warehouse? A gigantic locomotive for certain, but why? And why armed men, escorting it to and from the building in the middle of the night. A building that had been penetrated by someone who was as determined as he was to get a look inside.

First, he couldn't afford to be taken by the armed men. They wanted nothing more than to pistol whip him to death. Especially if they thought he was a poor wretch living week by week. He'd do better as a gentleman. And with the owners or managers of the company, his persona of a rich engineer might well be a perfect Trojan Horse. Then he might get the information he needed.

If they were answering to Hetzel, then he would finally have the confrontation he wanted – part of his plan to be on the offensive. If not, then why were they interested in him? There could be a thousand answers to that question. Asian Pacific and Southern. There was his old, well founded prejudice: anything of the South was suspect to him. Was this a situation that could prove his paranoia?

He tried to sleep. Occasionally he'd drift off but a noise or a shouting match would wake him eventually. It didn't matter. He felt ready if slightly weakened. He hadn't eaten, so he would need to spend a few of those precious nickels for a good meal. He had to make sure he wasn't going into a fight ill prepared.

It was time for Turner to attack. Yet, how would that work?

The park was quite lovely for that time of year, and if her long-time companion Miranda was not so intensely focused on the mission, she would have liked to have strolled along the lovely winding pedestrian path wrapped up in her fur coat.

There was nothing romantic about the park today.

A mist was clinging to the grass and slithering between the trees. Numerous birds chattered inside the protected enclosure of the foliage bordering the road and providing a canopy from the infrequent sun. It was cold and clammy. Rain was imminent. Perhaps snow. She could feel it in the air.

Couples promenaded, bundled up and clinging to each other with as much proper etiquette as the weather allowed. The fashionable of London were more likely over at Hyde Park, on Rotten Row, braving the cold, crowds, and each other. Here, things tended to be slightly less formal.

Miranda Gray, really Lettie's only female friend, was seated next to her, bundled up and grumbling quietly about not having finished breakfast. Surely Lettie understood what irritated her friend; that there were those in the world who committed atrocities and yet seemed to operate so freely in society that two women had to go to great lengths to confound them. Miranda grumbled in a resilient, mannerly way when she truly wished to rail or shout. She, like Lettie, preferred her adventures and confrontations to be direct and dynamic.

The barouche bounced down the Outer Circle road alongside Regents Park toward the southwest side where it was becoming more and more fashionable to live. These homes were not the expensive social repositories such as Belgrave Square or Mayfair. Late Georgian architecture in narrow, economic divisions, described the multi-story homes along such routes as Montagu Place and Baker Street. Modest, comfortable, confined ... and all those endless little staircases. Miranda's skin felt damp. An all too common consequence of living so close to a river. Fog was London's longest and most persistent resident.

"I'm certain that Sarah Bernhardt has ample rehearsal time before she performs to an audience. I should only wonder why we are not afforded such a significant detail?" Miranda squirmed in her seat, at once grumbling and growing excited by the prospect of their secretive activities.

"We neither of us are the Divine Sarah?"

"Touché."

"Consider this our opening show. If I fail on my part, I'll have a sight more to deal with than a bad review and closure of my play."

"I can think of no one more capable," Miranda said, perking up. She was in so many ways Lettie's sister, both in physical appearance and demeanor.

Miranda Gray was well situated having inherited a relative fortune and made a few pennies herself as a novelist in the last year or so, though she would never admit it. She wrote penny dreadfuls and melodramas under a *nom de plume* based off of her initials since no respectable lady wrote popular thrillers. M.R. Gray sounded like any man who had a sense of adventure and a way with words. No one seemed to care that the heroines of those novels were rather independent and all the heroes always had a good grasp of science. Really, she ought to be a publisher too, she said often. She would have to use this outing in one of her upcoming releases.

If they managed not to make fools of themselves.

If they managed not to get *killed* – which was, according to Lettie, a distinct possibility.

Lettie had been extremely frank about the situation and its risks. She pushed back the curtain with her left hand, slightly, so as to see and not be seen. Lettie had indeed informed her of everything except the danger of falling in love with a wild American man, whom she would never see again. According to Lettie, he was near to a paragon of virtue, with the exception of being an occasional thief, bully, and kidnapper. Poor Lettie, she'd explained all that away as if it wasn't an indication of his character and provided every excuse for his behavior that he himself would not have thought up.

Yet, she envied her friend. So many disappointments had come and gone in her own life. At least Lettie had an adventure or two in the wide world, and met a man who probably would have charmed Miranda too. Now, Lettie was including her – at the most dangerous point of the adventure, of course.

"One more time," she said with authority. "We are on a morning constitutional, you and me. The weather does not permit us a stroll so here we are in a barouche, circling Regents Park and the surrounding neighborhoods."

"Correct." Lettie peered out her window, making certain her face was seen. "I see more coaches and riders than walkers, so we are in the average with our behavior."

"The weather is cold, so you are wearing that lovely cloak – I gave you that, yes, never mind – with its large hood. So very reasonable. Fashionable too. Very good taste."

"Correct again." Lettie smiled – her friend's humor was comforting.

"As we pass by Baker Street, on our way home, you will leap out of a moving vehicle, leaving your cloak behind for me to prop up as though you are still here. You will rush into this man's quarters – I must say I'm not comfortable with that – before anyone can see what you've done. Remind me, Lettie dear, how a geologist learned all these covert and thrilling techniques?"

"Running for my life from a mad scientist?"

"Naturally," Miranda replied blandly. She was terribly excited but could never show it, not even to Lettie.

The barouche turned onto Park road and began following the park boundary. A man leaned against a lamp post, lighting a cigarette or cigar.

Her friend suddenly leaned forward, lips parted as if ready to call out to the man. Her face had become so pale, Miranda was sure it was this fellow, Turner.

Lettie had told her of Turner, in Paris, in Dover, following her. He had been leaning against a lamp post, lighting one of those cheroot cigars, trying to watch and yet not be seen. He had done the same in the Kent countryside, near Christopher Moore's home. It was an observational technique he used. Here again, a man waited in the fog. It couldn't be Turner, could it? She pushed her head to peek over Lettie's shoulder. "What is it?" she demanded.

"It can't be … Tom …"

"Mr. Turner? Here?"

As they neared the lamp post, Lettie raised her hand to thump on the roof – a signal to the driver to stop.

Her hand froze in place.

The man tried not to be seen, but failed. He obviously wasn't as good at it as Turner was.

Her friend's face flushed.

The Elegant Man had an accomplice – a dreadful creature he called Marcus who had manhandled Lettie in the hotel corridor, in Java. A foul man whose description made her skin crawl. Was it him? It *was* Marcus, wasn't it? He matched Lettie's portrayal to the letter.

Lettie fell back in her seat, allowing Miranda another chance to look. Miranda then glanced out the back. She wanted a good look at this fellow – to memorize his face, hands, anything that might give warning of his presence. "Not the Elegant Man?"

"No. His man."

"Then we know where he is and it isn't on Baker Street."

Down to earth, solid as a brick, that was Miranda. Lettie smiled. "Yes, we know where he is. We don't know if he has other accomplices but I have a suspicion that the Elegant Man prefers to work with a limited staff. I think he would have brought them as a show of force to scare me back in Java if he had the resources or the desire."

"They got here awfully quick."

"We can't underestimate the resources that Monsieur Hetzel has. He was able to secure the services of Captain Nemo, to get us from Spain to Holland in two days. While I would trust the Captain with my life, I don't doubt that Hetzel can talk most good people into doing his bidding without even knowing they are."

Miranda settled back in her side of the coach. "I should like to meet this Nemo. I read Jules Verne's biography. He sounds quite horrible and yet you describe him in better terms. Wait, here's Baker Street."

"What I wouldn't give to have my old Henry rifle," Lettie half whispered as she slipped the cloak from her shoulders and grasped her valise.

"If we manage to survive this insane idea of yours, I will see what I can arrange about that." Miranda watched out the back of the barouche for anyone following them. "I have my own resources. Can't write about gun fights without knowing a thing or two."

The street was mildly populated, with a low hanging haze of

leftover fog. Perfect to disguise her movement. The driver carefully steered around a large delivery cart and came close to the walkway, slowing as instructed. As the numbers increased toward 221, Lettie unlocked the door. A pair of thumps from the driver's heel on the base of his seat gave her the signal. A brief touch on the shoulder was Miranda's way of saying she would watch for her. Lettie pulled a veil down over her face from her hat and held her breath.

The barouche never stopped but it was lumbering along at the pace that she could step away from. The motion was smooth until Lettie's feet actually struck the paving halting yet all her momentum kept moving. A few wobbly steps carried her up onto the walkway, and three more swept her into the doorway of the building, out of Miranda's sight. One couple looked surprised but did nothing more that give that polite nod that one gave when neither words nor actions fit the moment.

As the barouche slid behind the lingering shroud of fog, the door opened and Lettie found herself safely inside 221 Baker with a singular hope and a valise full of fear.

The windows were slightly ajar, since Holmes had insisted on smoking two cigarettes during breakfast. It was, therefore, easy to hear a cab stop outside the front entrance to 221 Baker Street. Watson was too excited and stood up as the clopping sound of horses approached. The vehicle did not stop, and though Watson thought he heard a door slam shut, he sat down to wait a bit more.

"You've read the biographical pamphlet already, I gather, Watson?"

"Indeed I have."

Holmes's hand went out to receive the pamphlet as though at last ready to make some grand preparation for their visitor.

Watson held it back. "No, no, old cock; let me read the better parts. Ah … Doctor Gantry lectured between 1877 and 1882 on subjects pertaining to Volcanology and Mathematical Structures applicable to theoretical prediction models. The Doctor's," he changed the description from what he was reading, "work in geology on behalf of the Royal Academy of Sciences is noted. Saw Krakatoa go off it appears."

Mrs. Hudson, the landlady, could be heard chatting sweetly at the visiting professor as they climbed the stairs.

"Our professor is not a very large person," Holmes said, his face showing a momentary confusion. "In fact, he is extremely quiet." Turning to Watson and raising an eyebrow, "you have left something out?"

"You're the detective, old boy. You tell me." Watson was grinning from ear to ear.

The housekeeper opened the door and announced, "Doctor Gantry to see you Mr. Holmes." She was smiling too. They both, Hudson and Watson, were downright grinning.

Damn them both, they had known. Holmes could never

allow himself to admit he hadn't seen this coming, but he normally wasn't very interested in women, not even the woman he finally recognized from the newspapers. Frankly, as there was only one female Volcanologist in all of Great Britain and Europe, he had not even considered the possibility that out of the hundreds of such academics the one arriving in his parlor would be her. Watson could never know that.

"Doctor Gantry, come in," Holmes said as if he was completely informed. "May I inquire as to your satisfaction with your new position at New College?" Yes, he wouldn't give Watson the satisfaction. He had read about the woman and his brain simply abounded with details from the newspaper... now that he knew who had arrived on his doorstep.

Lettie swept into the room in a soft cloud of rose-based perfume and petticoats. She had arrived exceptionally dressed, though in a severe manner, and a little out of breath. Her head was held high, which allowed the light to reflect off her shiny black hair, swept up as it was, in the latest style. Her face, however, was covered with a dense net that allowed some indication of her features, to be hinted at rather than seen. And for some reason, she had no outer coat. She stepped forward and forcefully extended her hand, which still had a bit of a tremor to it. "Thank you, Mr. Holmes, for seeing me." Turning to Watson, she offered him a good handshake. "May I presume you are Dr. John Watson?"

"Indeed, Madame. I am at your service."

"As am I," Holmes interrupted. "Pray, be seated Miss ..."

"Doctor Gantry," she said without emotion. "Or simply Doctor, if you prefer." She hardly needed to tell him that he could call her by her title, but she liked the idea of reminding new male acquaintances that she would not be referred to as a spinster. And, she was nervous.

"Or perhaps 'Professor' would be best?"

"Not yet, Mr. Holmes. Not yet."

Once seated she opened a valise, which had been concealed behind her skirts and was overstuffed with papers, and quickly found what she was looking for. She handed him cut out articles from newspapers. Quietly, Holmes looked over each sheet. References to the Krakatoa eruption and the remarkable incident attributed to a mysterious airship.

Lettie noted the shaking in her hands, squeezed them quickly into fists, and then did everything possible to make them appear relaxed. The less time she spent there, the better. It was a terrible risk she was taking.

Unusually, she did not lift the veil off of her face. This Holmes found very intriguing. Why would she hide her face? Was she embarrassed to be known as "that woman scientist" in public – perhaps she'd suffered some sort of scorn she did not wish repeated? "There was some urgency to your request, Doctor?"

"Indeed." Now there was a quiver in her voice and she felt ashamed. The woman who survived Krakatoa should have more courage.

"Yet your need for an appointment was not urgent enough that it could not wait for two days?"

"This meeting had to suffer the impediment, Mr. Holmes, as there was no possible way for me to convey this matter other than in person, and there was a necessary delay in my coming to you. To be direct, I need your assistance in finding someone whom I believe to be in danger of losing his life. I read the American papers every day when I can find them, thoroughly expecting to learn that he has been murdered. I should hope that you can help me prevent such a thing from happening."

"Well, that is quite direct," Watson quipped, not intentionally meaning to sarcastic.

"Pray continue, Doctor."

"If you will allow me a little flattery, I came here because of your successes and because you are known to be discreet. I have nothing abhorrent to hide, I assure you. But I must inform you that there is a danger to your taking my case. I am being followed. The threat has been made that should I attempt to contact this gentleman in America, I and anyone else involved will be dealt with harshly. I will not fool myself into thinking my feminine state or my position in academia will protect me from anything they might chose to do to me. Hence, I am here, on my usual day of appointments and visits in the city, doing my best to conceal my true mission."

"In short Doctor, you wish others to have no knowledge that I might accept you as a client?"

"Absolutely none. I do not want these men to be aware of my actions, and not merely for my own sake. This is for your safety as

49

well. As I said, I have not done anything that should be considered improper – perhaps imprudent but never improper."

He tapped his fingers against one another – an annoying habit Watson disliked in Holmes. "To your colleagues and neighbors you may feel free to say whatever comes to mind. However to me, you must lay forth every detail, most especially if my safety, yours, or any other's is in jeopardy. Why is it you feel you are being followed?" His tone was unintentionally dismissive.

Watson squirmed in his seat and grimaced slightly.

Lettie leaned in, somewhat insulted. "Mr. Holmes, I will tell you everything, for I think it will take every detail to accomplish the task. I have no intention of lying to anyone but would prefer not to discuss the matter in the first place with strangers. The less they know, the less *they* are at risk. As to my concerns, I believe the data will support my conclusion."

"Very well." Holmes's eyes opened wide, but he gave no other outward signs.

"I am requesting your help in finding a man who was a former naval intelligence officer for the United States and is rather good at what he was trained to do. I last saw him being taken in a stretcher to an American vessel, the *Abraham Lincoln*, bound for San Francisco. He was injured during the eruption of Krakatoa and I felt he should be removed back to his own homeland to encourage his return to health. A simple and logical decision."

Scowling, Holmes stared at her. "If he is in America, what do you expect me to do from London?"

Lettie wouldn't let him off so quickly. "A good researcher always has multiple forms of information. Detective work is very similar, yes? In fact, they are one and the same. But in your case, you have what I do not: contacts of a specific sort – shall we say, non-scientific? Contacts no lady would normally have. I would be disappointed, Mr. Holmes, if you did not have a number of close connections in America who can make quiet inquires on your behalf."

"Why go to such troubles for a man who should be quite capable of seeing to himself, in his own country?"

"I became rather *fond* of him. That he survived such a horrible event is nothing short of miraculous. That any of us did ..." Her voice tapered off as images of the coast of Java filled her thoughts. Holmes and Watson had no idea what she'd seen. Bodies lying on the beach, some floating in the water. She felt her eyes watering simply thinking of it all. Yet she couldn't allow either man to dismiss her emotions as womanly weakness, thus she kept her face hidden beneath the veil. "After I arranged for Mr. Turner to go aboard the *Lincoln*, I went back to work on the remains of the island. I am, after all, a volcanologist and must put my skills to work. A few days later, it was determined by a committee of scientists that my efforts should not be needed – certainly not at the eruption site where I might … embarrass some members of the academic community who feel that a woman should never be endangered for the sake of science."

For the first time since the meeting began, Holmes sat up properly, ceased his eccentric behavior, and seemed to look on Lettie differently. Never with the level of appreciation he might show a male mathematician or chemist, but certainly with a new level of respect for a woman.

"He sounds as though he was in excellent hands and headed to America. I gather he is happy to see America again? Yes? Of course. But why do you now fear for his life?"

"Because … he was first mate aboard a remarkable airship." She pointed to an article regarding the mystery cloud ship. "And while he obeyed his commander unquestioningly, he came to understand that the Captain's genius came with a cost … insanity. To make this short, the ship crashed and Mr. Turner was the only surviving crewman."

"Surely that isn't enough to think the man is in danger?" Holmes was actually trying not to sound condescending. "Or that you are still embroiled in his dangers?"

Lettie looked up. "Before I left Java, I was accosted by two men and a threat was made against me: I must not contact Mr. Turner, else I would face severe consequences. I decided, foolishly I'm sure you'll think, to discover who these scoundrels were. I do have a few of my own contacts who have resources … I learned that they work for Pierre Jules Hetzel, a French businessman."

Holmes sat up at the name.

"I see you recognize the name."

"Indeed!"

She stood up and paced near the fireplace. It was clean but somehow cluttered, even for a man's apartment. Perhaps, by the number of packed items, they had not yet settled. "There are advantages to being on excellent terms with a Reuters correspondent. I don't have all the facts here Mr. Holmes, but one thing I know is that Monsieur Hetzel wished to have those marvelous inventions. In fact, he sent two men to follow me and to see what I know. And … by logic one must ask, if he sent men to follow me, what would he do to get his hands on the first mate? I don't know how much Mr. Turner knows, but I suspect not nearly so much as the world would like him to. I fear that any protest of ignorance on his part will be considered deception. I am terrified that such men, in search of riches or power …"

"… or both …"

"… yes, or both, will torture and then murder Mr. Turner. It was certainly intimated to me that they would never allow Mr. Turner to live no matter what. Having returned home, I have now seen those men in the theater, possibly even in coming here today – I believe." She turned to face both men. "I am not prone to hyperbole, Mr. Holmes. I am fully aware that my ordeal of the last year may have caused me to be too sensitive. I am, however, certain that I am being followed. As to Mr. Turner …yes, I am fond of this man but can assure you that I have not maintained any connection beyond a wish of a happy and healthy life for him. Mr. Holmes, please – He is a good man, and I fear that we cannot spare any more good men in light of the madmen and war mongers who seem to be on the rise."

"And how shall any of us know him?"

"He is average in height but very strongly built. Brown hair and remarkably intense, blue eyes. That alone should not distinguish him. He has a scar on his throat. It was made when the Confederacy had imprisoned him in a war camp and tried to execute him. Apparently, Death did not take to him, nor he to it."

"He's a lucky man. He may well still be lucky."

"But a bit friendless. All his connections were on board that airship and all perished when she crashed. I need to be his friend in a prudent manner. He needs help, Mr. Holmes. I am convinced of this. The data entirely supports my conclusion."

For a bit of time, Holmes paced where she had. Once, he walked to the window and looked out past a sweep of curtains. "Doctor Gantry, you believe this man is worth saving?"

"Yes."

"Then I shall make inquiries. I will need a detailed account of your business in the Indies. And, I believe it will be necessary that you provide me with accurate descriptions of the men following you."

Lettie stood up. "Do you see someone, on the street?"

Holmes glanced down again at the busy street. "Calm yourself, Doctor, I see no one whom I would suspect of watching these rooms. But, having such information will be vital if I am to make certain that you are safe."

Watson felt a rush of relief race down into his chest. Holmes was quite serious about the lady's case.

"You needn't spend a moment worrying about me. It is Mr. Turner who is most likely in immediate danger and I would request you place your greatest skills in his defense." She clasped her hands at her waist. "Without causing you undue danger, how can we communicate?"

Holmes almost danced with delight, as though such a secretive and dangerous case was a game. "Are you lecturing regularly?"

"Indeed. Every Tuesday afternoon."

"Then it would seem that both Doctor Watson and I are to return to school. As I am known to attend lectures and performances at New College, it will not be out of place for me to do so now."

Lettie stared at the carpets for a moment, drew in a deep breath and met his gaze with equal determination. "Thank you, Mr. Holmes. And you, Doctor Watson."

"Watson, what do you make of it all?" Holmes pushed back the curtain gently, allowing for an opening that gave him a view of a barouche on the street. The moment it arrived, Doctor Gantry dashed out of her front door and climbed into the enclosure. Neither the driver nor the occupant attempted to help her. And for a brief moment, Holmes swore he saw petticoats over the feet of the passenger. Another woman? "So much fuss," he muttered.

Watson draped himself back across the sofa and stared at the ceiling, drawing on his cigarette. "She seems genuinely concerned for this Yankee, and for her own life."

"'Concerned?' Watson, she is terrified. But the question is not her emotional state or her sincerity in her *belief* that she is being threatened. These things I do not doubt. The question at hand is whether there is a real threat."

Sitting up with an appalled expression, Watson put out the cigarette with significant force. "Old boy, I think you may have become an example of those habits you criticize in the police – namely you are assuming." When Holmes' shock was apparent, he continued easily. "You are assuming that she is governed by fear and emotion and would therefore be unduly fretful of imaginary threats. She struck me as quite logical. It is my opinion that if she is afraid, she had deduced that such fear is warranted."

Holmes slowly returned his gaze to the street, now empty, below. "For the sake of the lady, I hope she is wrong."

December 1883
Market Street and Mason
San Francisco, California

"Good God Almighty. Is that really *you*, Turner?" The younger man stepped out of the shadows where he had been waiting. It wasn't particularly unusual for a uniformed, naval officer to be lurking around the area — there were certainly plenty of sailors wandering about the saloons and brothels — but he'd been asked to have a care for his safety. His hand rested on a shiny, new, small caliber pistol deep in his coat pocket; it was only logical.

Turner pushed his hat back and allowed the light from a gas lamp to show all his features. In a gesture he would never otherwise make, he allowed his scar to be seen as though it were a verification of his identity. The naval man was cautious at first, until he saw the discolored skin. "Hello Ben Willey. How the hell are you?" He stuck out his hand, never so glad to have seen another human being.

Willey snagged his hand and pulled him into a big warm hug. Slapping his friend appreciatively on the back, he kept vigorously shaking Turner's hand until Turner was able to politely extricate himself. "I can't believe it's you. In fact I was sure it couldn't be. You'd bucked the odds so many times, my bet was that someone got awfully lucky and you were dead."

"Been close."

"I'd ask you what you've been up to the past few years, but as you know," he swept his hand across his naval uniform, "that is a topic I am up to date on. You'll have to catch me up on the last couple of months though, that's about where I lost track of you."

Turner couldn't help himself. He shoved his hands into his pockets and stared at the ground until he could let go of some of his shame. It was all fine and jolly that civilians knew he had a past, but for a friend and fellow officer, the infamy was almost unbearable. "I won't bother you with some excuse about doing what a man has to, to survive."

Shaking his head, Willey didn't seem too worried about explanations. "And I won't bother you with a lie by saying I don't understand myself. But bloody hell, Turner, did you have to go sign up with a lunatic? And how did you get mixed in with all those kidnappings? Please tell me that madman was holding you hostage too."

The label thrust onto Robur's name truly bothered him. "He wasn't insane when I met him. Robur was plenty of things I wish he wasn't ... hadn't been ... but at the time, he seemed the sanest man around." He pulled up his collar and settled the cap back down on his forehead as the mist turned into an earnest rain. "No excuses for me, but I can explain if you need it. At this point I have no intention of avoiding the truth. Lose the coat, Commander, and let me buy you a drink."

"I'm going to need it, aren't I," Willey said, removing his uniform coat and hat. In shirt sleeves and waistcoat, he looked like nearly everyone else around the area, though perhaps cleaner. He had the ubiquitous moustache and slicked-back hair that younger officers sported these days. Though taller than Turner, Willey was rail thin and not particularly athletic. He was by nature and occupation a clerk. An Annapolis graduated clerk whose papers were of extreme sensitivity.

They chose the first saloon that didn't have a pile of disreputable men sleeping outside. It was too early in the evening for most of the crowd to have arrived, so Turner and Willey had their choice of seats, close to the cast-iron stove. The comfortable aroma of spilled and somewhat over-cooked coffee was at odds with the place.

Out of habit, they both checked who was seated within hearing range. Turner strolled up to the bar, purchased a quarter-full bottle and two glasses.

"I'd only play with that glass of ... whatever it is they call whiskey." Willey said dismissively as Turner began to pour.

"Oh, I know. Something about the contents?"

"Or perhaps the container? Sanitation is not a high mark in these waters." He rested his arms on the table and leaned as close as he could to Turner. "Beard and moustache look good on you. You could almost pass for a flag officer."

Turner ignored the comment. "I was glad when I read in the

paper that you were assigned out here."

"Only just," Willey said.

"Just last week or just admitting that you've been here for a spell?"

Willey smiled, wondering just how disappointed he would have been if Turner hadn't questioned the stated facts. "Officially, I've been here a week. That is the official statement from my office. Now, why did you contact me? I'm glad to play catch-up, hell we haven't seen each other in over a decade, but I doubt you're interested in chit-chat. You don't do things by half. What's going on in that mind of yours, Turner?"

"Touché. I have some information that you need to know. Perhaps you know all this already and I'll just bore you for a bit. But I don't like the idea that you might not be aware of something so potentially dangerous. Let's start with the fact that I caught the attention of some gentlemen. Don't ask how ... no, actually, please don't ask. Southerners. Rich Southerners." The tone in his voice surprised him. He wasn't used to speaking about anyone with such anger ... such hatred. Yes, hatred was accurate. He hadn't realized it, but in the quiet of the empty saloon, sensitive to his words with Willey listening, he heard it.

"Are you letting the war haunt you again, Turner?" Willey tilted his head, as though seeing Turner differently. He couldn't blame him. "Christ, it ended almost twenty years ago." He couldn't help but look at Turner's scar. Of course Turner was obsessed.

Turner avoided Willey's stare – he was used to it by now. "I considered that. Lord knows I can't seem to get away from it. No, there was something odd about them. First off, they sent someone to spy on me - to follow me."

"Which you evaded, of course."

"Of course, and I followed *him* instead."

"Of course. What did you find, Turner?" When Turner didn't immediately reply, Willey felt his muscles tightening. His friend was prone to a bit of reasonable paranoia, but what he'd learned was scaring him – he could tell by the expression on Turner's face. What scared Turner, terrified Willey. "Tom?"

Turner leaned back and checked his environment a second time. Two working girls waiting for paying customers, hopefully to dance and nothing more. The barkeeper was arranging his glasses, bottles and a sawed-off shotgun for greater efficiency. A drunk was thrown back against his chair and he sat snoring with a wide-open mouth. In a little over an hour, the place would be filled to the line with cast-offs from the Barbary Coast. "I found a building owned by the Asian Pacific and Southern company."

Willey's eyes widened, but otherwise he maintained a calm exterior. He took a second look at the room, for safety's sake.

"That's what I thought, Ben. You've heard that name before, haven't you?"

"Yes." Why bother lying? Turner would know if he was. "You went inside, didn't you?"

"Of course."

"Should be careful about that. Men get shot for trespassing on businesses. They get mistaken for thieves, saboteurs, or industrial spies."

"So I discovered."

That caught Willey' attention more than ever. "You're not hurt ..."

"No," Turner replied, holding up a hand. "No. I simply discovered that fact."

"What did you find?"

"Getting serious now?"

"Very. Tom, what the hell did you find?"

"A locomotive."

"It is a transportation company. Trains, ships, the standard modes."

Turner smiled in his lopsided way. "I see you do know about them. This locomotive is unlike anything I've ever seen. I've been on the French and British rail systems, and I've seen some of their fancier designs. Nothing like this. Has to be at least a quarter to a half bigger than a standard passenger engine. Everything is blued or dulled, so it won't reflect light. It's using an odd combination of chemical lights, electricity, and liquid fuel. Doesn't smell or act like a basic locomotive. And ... it doesn't sound like one. Quiet, in relative terms. It's not noisy."

Willey thought for a few moments. "Standard track gauge?"

Turner nodded.

"What's its hauling capacity?"

For that, Turner had no answer. "I didn't get close enough

58

before they were on me. But the sheer size suggest impressive performance."

"I need you to get me more information."

"Willey – I can't stay here. It's a long story but right now, I'm on the move. There's a risk for anyone who is near. Has nothing to do with mystery trains or suspect companies. Please accept that I can't remain in place for very long. It's not *my* life I'm worried about."

"I can't say much myself, but let me tell you that this is an issue that will affect your country. *Your country*, damn it Turner. You've stumbled onto something bigger than you know. The problem is, I can't tell you how big – because I don't know myself. We've been getting word that someone is planning an attack, probably in the next year."

"Hence the pretense that you just got here, but were here checking on things for a while?"

"Yes." He was asking too much of his friend and he knew it. "We need to learn more. These 'gentlemen' who took an interest in you. Do you know why? Do you recognize any of them?"

Shaking his head, he wondered how bad he was about to look. "No names were ever exchanged. They thought I was an engineer from England." Slowly, he stood up, facing his friend. "I've given you what I know. I'm sorry that it isn't more. If your sources are right and no one is making their move until the new year, then you have some time. I won't ask what your sources are saying about who or what is being planned. But I do believe if you go to the warehouse, you'll learn a great deal."

Willey huffed a little. "I already have. Only the locomotive wasn't there when I checked. Your good luck; you got to see it."

"So you're the one who left the coal door unlocked and chipped a hole in the foundation."

"Did you find it useful?" Willey's voice seemed cheered by the prospect.

"Saved my life." Turner offered him his hand. "See here, Willey. If I learn more, I won't hold back. You know me – I won't keep something like this to myself. But that's all I can give you." As Willey stood up, looking to protest, Turner added, "That's all I can."

"I know. You're a good man, Tom Turner. I don't know everything that happened to you after the war. But ... we didn't do right by our veterans. I honestly feel ashamed when I think about it."

"You shouldn't. Not your fault in the least and you certainly weren't the one in charge."

"I'm part of all this. I was just going into Annapolis when the war ended. I remember taking down your testimony at the Henry Wirz trial. And 'the Investigation'," he said with a knowing glance.

"You can be such a clerk, can't you?"

"As the only man in Washington with legible handwriting, I had every officer and military lawyer scrambling to make me a better offer. I think I like the choice I made, but sometimes I feel like I earned my rank on the graves of men who fought bravely. I have yet to see actual battle."

Turner set his hand on the young man's shoulder. "You didn't. You were simply, proverbially, in that right place and time. And I don't doubt you earned every inch you've gained."

"It'll be good to work with you again."

"Someday. One never knows. But not today."

He scolded himself all the way out of the saloon and down Market Street. He was such a liar. All it took was seeing the face of a colleague who didn't think ill of him, who begged him to serve his country again. Poor Ben, he didn't understand that no one in Washington wanted Turner back. Still ... why would such a little thing like that slow him down? He was, as he had promised himself, on the offensive. If not against Hetzel, then against locomotive builders with dubious intentions and southern drawls. It wasn't fair of him to judge a Southern man more harshly than a Northern one, but in this case he wasn't mistaken.

December 1883
The Point Lobos Toll Road
San Francisco, California

A storm was gathering a few miles off shore, holding back until it had the strength to overwhelm the warm air above the land and push into the California landscape, pounding against the Sierras. Between rare gaps in the clouds, shafts of white and gray light poured down onto the unpaved road.

At a lower elevation to the south stretched the newest roads through the sand dunes to Ocean Beach and Golden Gate Park. From his perch higher up the hill, Turner could stop and take in a great deal of his surroundings. It was temporarily comforting for a man who usually wondered what awaited him behind every boulder. The trees on the high cliff and hills were stooped over from the constant wind and frequent tempests, creating a feeling of being in a tunnel.

A horse drawn buggy thundered by on the north-side speed track, headed back to the city. From the amount of mud and sand caked on the vehicle, it was clear that the young man driving it had been racing down at the beach. Certainly the young woman clinging to his arm and shrieking with glee at the dangerous speed at which they were travelling thought much of the situation.

He'd been warned by the hotel clerk that the Cliff House was for common folk and riff-raff, and the occasional meeting of business men who required "special privacy." It had been a high class restaurant and place to be seen, but the building had slowly become a meeting place for undesirables and newly moneyed persons, who did not know yet that they could now afford better manners. The higher class customer had been driven away. Seemed to Turner that this was not such a bad place for him, but in his finest imitation of Lettie's accent, he had explained he was only interested in the view. And he was. He wanted to see why the men from the Asian Pacific and Southern company risked their business reputations by going there for meetings.

Turner had been invited to one of those meetings. He had declined politely. He was only pretending to be a railroad engineer, and had no intention of being questioned on points he could never answer.

The old toll booth was empty. It seemed that the company which built the road and charged for passage could not maintain such demands on the public wallet when newer, cleaner roads had been built parallel to it. The booth reminded him of an abandoned shack, ready to welcome every ghost that wandered up from shipwrecks on the coast. The blowing wind created a low groan as it pushed its way through the rotting boards and trembling, shattered windows.

Turner kept walking, sweeping his cane as if nothing in the world was bothering him and he'd come to take his evening constitutional. Twice, he had to press his hat onto his head as the wild wind tried to snatch it away.

Ahead of him, he could see that trees were not abundant. What few there were had been cleared to make way for the road. The closer he got to the end of it, nearer to the ocean, the fewer living things seemed to thrive. A wave of sand blew up and past him. The road itself was slick and muddy. Turner kept walking. His left hand rested in his overcoat pocket on the grip of one of his Navy Colts. His knuckles brushed against a pair of spyglasses that were no bigger than a pair of opera glasses yet twice as powerful. Now and then, as he was certain someone was looking, he stopped to take in the scenery.

A cart drove by with several loud, celebrating folks, all headed back into San Francisco.

For the most part, he was alone.

The smell of the sea began to blow past him along with grit and gravel. It was a familiar and pleasant scent for a sailor. Turner took in a deep breath, noting the additional aromas of plants, burned material, and yes … a few horses.

By the time he reached the end of the road, or rather where it made a sharp turn south and down toward the beach far below, he'd abandoned any pleasantries of his environment and heightened his sense of awareness. From the top of the cliff, he could see the old building propped up on the basalt cliff. Barking seals called out to one another from a substantial rock formation just beyond the building.

The Cliff House was rather plain. Two stories of restaurant, rooms, and viewing decks topped by a peaked roof. A flag whipped in the wind but had been there for so long that its colors were indiscernible at a distance. There were only a few lights on. Some carriages, traps, buggies, or horses waited near the entrance but did not indicate a large crowd. Most of the people who had come out to play had abandoned their fun at the sight of the growing storm. Only the most determined diner would stay. Or … businessmen who preferred the lack of tourists.

Waves were pounding the shore and the cliff – the incoming storm was shoving the ocean ahead of it. Surges of water slammed into the rocks and sprayed up into the air. Even the seals were beginning to abandon their precarious rock.

The hill descending to the Cliff House was difficult yet not unmanageable in the darkening light. Turner crouched down and held his glasses up to his eyes. No movement inside. There was a chance that none of the men he sought were present. If so, he'd wasted an afternoon and would likely get soaked by the rain on his way back.

No, they had invited him to join their gathering; they would be there.

Carefully, he climbed down the embankment nearest the northeast corner of the building. His hands rested on the cold stone of the foundation as he carefully stepped around toward a window facing the ocean.

Peering through the window he could see an empty restaurant. The chairs stacked atop of the tables as though the business had not opened. That was strange. The sign he passed out front stated meals every afternoon and evening except for Mondays. It was Sunday.

A burst of laughter from the second story made him jump slightly but he knew that it was far more likely that businessmen would have a room of their own to dine in. Had they arranged for the restaurant to be closed? That was expensive.

Turner found the kitchen door. Unlocked. Stranger by the moment. The kitchen itself was cold and dark. No one had planned on serving meals. The three stoves were freshly blackened but their fires unlit. Plateware was stored away.

The corridor leading toward the entrance to the Cliff House was also dark, but lights from the staircase give him enough to see by.

Every footstep was placed carefully, with Turner listening for a squeak in the flooring or the click of a door handle being turned. Every breath was shallow.

More laughter from above.

The smell of cigars.

The aroma of mold.

The rattle of the windows by the wind.

The stairs did not creak under him as he climbed up the carpeted sections, slowly and carefully. The second floor was better appointed. One needed more importance to make use of the rooms here, and thus they reflected the better wealth of such persons.

Turner grasped his Colt by the grip but kept it hidden.

One door was ajar, brighter light coming from within. This was obviously the room where the laughter came from. Men's laughter. But he couldn't make out anyone's voice in particular. Turner stayed back and quickly looked for a place to hide should he need it.

The voices were in a pleasant conversation but the words were not quite clear enough. The genial chatter was punctuated by the occasional laugh or exuberant agreement.

He pressed his back against the same wall as the room ahead. He could almost make out the words. The accents? Yes, that particular deep Southern drawl that reminded him too much of the past. He'd found them. Turner waited. Patiently, he could wait to hear what he needed to.

The voices abruptly stopped.

He heard the clicking of a hammer drawing back.

Ah, the Turner luck had failed. Well, he wanted to hear what they were talking about. Now he would. What could he tell them that would make sense? How would he explain his presence when he'd declined the meeting? And he was sneaking up on the room, as the man behind him would testify.

"Mister Turner. I am so glad y'all decided to join our meeting."

Turner? He'd never told them that name. Oh hell.

Late November 1883
Residence of L. Gantry
Sutton, Surrey, England

Late in the afternoon, the third of four daily postal deliveries arrived. It had six invitations for dinner, a thick letter from her father, and a single note.

Have looked into the details of your lecture and find neither data to support your conclusion nor has the American professor returned inquires for the same. I am therefore unwilling to continue to explore your hypothesis until such time as more definitive data can be provided. I apologize for any inconvenience but I must decline further consideration. My colleague continues to have an interest and may, from time to time, attend a lecture when his schedule permits. S.H.

Lettie stared at the note, and felt her heart pounding enough to shake her. Despite the secretive wording of the note it was clear that Sherlock Holmes was abandoning her. He was abandoning Tom. She crumpled the note into a tight ball and in a moment of despair, flung it as hard as possible. A foolish thing, as the paper did not travel far and the explosion of frustration was weak and feeble. Just like a woman, she bemoaned softly, feeling both weak and feeble. Damnable men. Always men. Men had harmed her; nearly killed her. Men were selling weapons in massive attempts to glean profit from death. Men were creating mechanical monsters like Hetzel's minion Philip Wickham and unleashing them on the world. Men.

Not all men. Her father was not one of those who constantly betrayed and abandoned her. Neither was Christopher Moore. Reliable as the day was long in summer.

Yet she couldn't endanger them. They might have the sort of contacts she needed, but to ask them was to put them at enormous risk.

Ten years of demeaning comments about her person and her nature; endless discussions about her perceived lack of intelligence; kidnapping; Krakatoa; and now this. Lettie sat down and decided she would find a way to help Tom … on her own.

She needed her rifle … no, that was long gone, lost aboard the *Albatross*. She needed another. Irrationally, she wanted another model '62 Henry repeating rifle. Weapons technology had long since improved the gun but she liked that it had been used in a war to end slavery, or so many British citizens thought the war was about, and that death mongers like Wickham and Hetzel would think it too old fashioned to approve. Lettie didn't need their approval or their concepts of technological innovation. Besides, she was fairly good with *that* rifle.

Now she could concentrate on the work at hand. Fine, if Holmes had abandoned her, she would find another way. A message to Professor Flockmocker, who had been so helpful? He worked occasionally for Hetzel, which was how they met, but she'd never had the opinion that he was "Hetzel's man." And the Frenchman …

Professor Rajiv Pierce could help. He would know how to find Flockmocker, being a fellow inventor. She could arrange it so that Pierce was not endangered – he'd had enough of that over the last year. And … Pierce might not be so eager to assist Tom Turner, the man who had abducted them both for Captain Robur. Oh God, what a mess it was.

Perhaps Flockmocker could alert Nemo; to let him know what Hetzel was about. Maybe they could go to America …

She was getting ahead of herself. This would take the sort of planning and detail that she applied to a fact-finding excursion to an erupting volcano.

Slowly, Lettie turned up the lamp in her room as the light began to fade into nighttime. Taking out a sheet of paper, she began to list everything. Fears she would consider one at a time, with several outcomes. She was a scientist, damn it all! Logic would serve her, not emotion. Yet as she set her pen to paper, a sad feeling washed over her. What if she failed? What if she only led Hetzel to Tom?

December 1883
The Cliff House on Point Lobos
Outskirts of San Francisco, California

In the storm deadened light, the green walls were heavy and crushing, giving the "gentlemen's" room a claustrophobic sensation. Nothing was unpolished or undusted — rich men were never fond of dust. Every detail was in the correct place. Every detail *was* correct. Framed paintings hung on tasseled ropes from the picture rails. An entire saloon's worth of liquor was decanted in crystal and waited to be consumed by those who thought nothing of the expense. A dense cloud of cigar smoke clung to the ceiling — the aroma of many years had permeated the Persian carpets and pillows. Taxidermied animals sat staring at the membership.

He came looking — he had no one to blame but himself for getting caught. If Turner was smart, he could play his hand carefully and learn as much as possible.

The view through wide leaded windows was remarkable. The Pacific Ocean was partially obscured by the clouds that had now battled San Francisco's famous fog and won. To the south, the expanse of Ocean Beach stretched off into the shrouded basalt cliffs near Pacifica. A constant barking of seals echoed throughout the halls.

No one spoke.

Everyone observed.

Turner looked at the men seated in over-stuffed chairs of velvet and ebony. Most smoked and it reminded him that he had only a few of his beloved cheroot cigars remaining. It was unlikely that he would be offered anything.

His guard remained an impolite three feet away, as he had since the moment he'd put a gun to the back of Turner's head and escorted him into the room. There was something familiar and yet wrong about the man. What was it? A smell of fluid — hydraulic fluid? A slight creaking when he moved to match any shift Turner made in his weight? The blank, almost demonic stare that only one of Hetzel's improved minions had?

He'd walked into his worst nightmare. Willingly and wide-eyed. All the time thinking he was so clever.

Five men, himself, and the guard. None of the men initially appeared to be armed but that was difficult to confirm in the lowering light.

The men were so very comfortable in their surroundings that surely they had been there many times before, as he suspected.

Not wishing to be the first to speak, Turner began taking note of the painting nearest him. He knew the sort of place. A palatial white mansion with tall columns, the thick magnolia trees, and the idealized agrarian scene – bright with colors amongst the gray tones flushed into the room by an incoming storm. The silence was becoming ridiculous. "Should I attempt to maintain the identity I gave you?"

"I see no reason why y'all should go to such troubles. Do you recognize the place, Mister Turner?" There was a distinctive southern drawl in the question as if the speaker wanted to emphasize his birthright as he pointed toward the painting.

Turner did not bother to look back at the man and made no attempt at affecting the accent he had used previously. They were on to him. "Specifically, no. It is a plantation scene to be sure. Virginia? Carolinas?"

"South Carolina. The first state to bravely remove itself from the so-called Union."

Turner continued to keep his back to the man. "I suspect you know that I am not likely to use the word 'brave' in describing secession." He shifted his weight and his guard matched the movement.

"No, I suppose y'all wouldn't. But there are those of us who see it … differently."

"You do realize that the war ended two decades ago and that the Union remained intact? With some exceptions, everyone – North and South – seem to be doing reasonably well."

The man laughed. "In some ways y'all are correct. Though I will say with confidence that the last chapter of that saga has yet to be written."

Finally, slowly, Turner moved away from the painting and

faced the men in the room. They were seated, he was not. That gave them a small feeling of superiority but not a tactical advantage. If there were no firearms to be reached, he still had many options for weaponry. The letter opener on the table next to the man who spoke. Any of the crystal decanters that could shatter into sharp pieces. His own bare hands.

For the moment, none of those seemed to be necessary. Besides, he wasn't sure what he could do about the guard, especially if he was one of Hetzel's creations.

"You have the proverbial advantage: how do you know me? And who are you, if you are at all planning to tell me?"

"Call me Milton. I have been made aware of your wartime record and the unfortunate events in Georgia," he said, swiping his thumb across his throat, referencing Turner's scar which was well hidden beneath his high collar. "I cannot tell you how much I counted my luck when I understood who I had stumbled upon. But then, I have the greatest luck. And here I was, when I received a lovely gift from Paris, France," he indicated the guard, "and a document with such amazing information."

"And you thought it might be good business to accept this windfall?"

"Of course. To refuse Mr. Hetzel would be uncommonly foolish. Like Hetzel, I was involved in a devastating war yet emerged a businessman rather than a soldier.

"A common occurrence."

"Mister Turner. We," and Milton waved his cigar out toward the other fellows, "are a consortium of gentlemen who find ourselves in political, financial, an' philosophical agreement."

"Gentlemen's societies have been founded on less."

"Indeed, sir, indeed. However, persons such as yourself have been known to dislike our little …"

"… club?"

"One might say. Yes, our Gentleman's Club is unlike most others and therefore expects to be opposed. Violently opposed, I reckon."

"Don't you already have such an institution? Something about the Knights of something-or-other." Too many gangs of men, calling each other noble and honorable titles, trying to sound as though they were the inheritors of the grandeur of old. All they turned out to be were thugs, bullies, and con artists, North and South alike.

Milton didn't like the suggestion. "Those men like to talk. I prefer a man who takes to action. The words can come later." He was clearly unhappy with the comparison. "We are not, indeed most emphatically not, the Knights of the Golden Circle, nor the Sons of Liberty, nor those fools claiming to be. We are unique and new."

At first Turner looked at his shoes, not in shame but in an effort to hide an expression that belied amusement. He stared up at them, his blue eyes distinct even in the growing darkness. "Violence only begets violence – this was one of the hardest lessons of the war. I'm sure that businessmen of the West clearly understand that violence costs money and reduces profit."

"It depends on the business." Milton took a long drag on his cigar and pushed the smoke out of his mouth. "If one's business *is* violence, then such consequences only lead to greater profit, especially if the profit is not necessarily monetary. But we here, we are not war mongers out for gold. We have a purpose and know that hatred is a powerful motivator when the end goal is noble but difficult to achieve." He suddenly smiled and tamped out his cigar. Leaning forward, he clasped his hands over his knees. "I think we generally understand one another. My colleagues and I are of the belief that a war lost is not a goal lost – only a setback. It is our intention not to secede, as that proved unsuccessful. Our intention is to create."

"Your own Utopia?"

"Indeed. We will start from scratch a society that recognizes the primacy of the superior being, lives close to the land, and holds what God has given us dearly. Every citizen will know their proper place. There will be stability. Sanity. Order – proper order."

"If you are off to some uninhabited island to establish your society, I wish you good luck. I have no interest in joining you, as I'm sure that the superior being can only be represented by you, and laws will be applicable to everyone but you, and anyone who is not 'you' will be held in some form of contempt. That is no Utopia to my mind. Enjoy yourselves – I'll not stop you."

"I... yes ... well, here's where we have our collision of purpose. The only islands worthy of our society appear to be too well occupied and too many are eyeing it for themselves.

Turner couldn't help smiling. He folded his arms across his

chest as though it might protect his heart from what he anticipated to be the incoming barrage of horse shit to be flung at him. "You've therefore discounted the Kingdom of Hawai'i? Where then are you going and why should I care? Why should anyone care so long as you go? If you can't live here as a member of this society, then leave. No one needs you – go be happy somewhere else. Go enslave people to your heart's content, but don't be surprised if that doesn't last long. Some ideas have died off for good reason." He was being too sharp and had said too much, fully unable to stop his own prejudices in the matter.

A blond, bearded man stood up. "The war was never about slavery – it was about Northern aggression and the elimination of our way of life! You Northerners were strangling us, destroying our ability to survive, for nothing but greed!"

"Sit down Haverland. He's baitin' you and your logic will fall on deaf ears, won't they Turner? Abolitionist, Unionist, Republican. That is all Mister Turner here will accept."

Turner tilted his head to the left. "I thought we were talking about your Utopia and how you were leaving to go set it up?"

"Yes. We were. And ... I... here is our quandary: we're not going anywhere. This coast is just fine for our needs. Oregon to the Baja. Pacific Ocean to the Rockies. The New Confederacy. There aren't many civilized people here right now, so few will be disturbed if they are forced to leave for ideological reasons. I suspect many if not nearly all will agree with our prospect and will gladly join. I think y'all underestimate the lingering resentment from the war and the desire to achieve true order again. The South may not rise again, but its heart will continue beating as strong as ever."

Turner leaned back defensively as though being an inch closer would make him feel dirtied by Milton and his ilk. "The whole Western coast? That's asking a bit, don't you think?" He was angry and had no need to conceal it. It had been Southerners like Milton who gave him his scar, ruined his hopes and dreams, nearly destroyed his country. He thought he had, but he knew now he couldn't forgive so easily. "The Union won't allow you to cut us off from Western ports, silver and gold mining, and agriculture. You haven't the money, means, or man power to make a land grab of that size. And you're forgetting Mexico – they may not have the most stable government but they might easily unite to keep foreigners like you from stealing land – and some of their people too?"

"People will do the strangest things when motivated by fear. Let me tell y'all a little story about an astronomer named Jose Bonilla. August of last year he made the outrageous claim to have seen 300 dark objects in the Mexican skies. Everyone at the Zacatecas Observatory was certain he was seeing geese or some such thing that fell between the sun and his camera. But the hysteria that followed his unidentified heavenly bodies report stirred up the wildest behavior. Mass panic, religious fervor, rebellion against established authority." Milton stood up and swept the last of the curtains open. "Imagine what a fleet of *these* would do to the populace, especially if they hear that there are thousands more when this one came from? If a white man with a pistol could take over an island, I believe we can do far more." He gestured at the window.

Powerful hands clamped down on Turner's shoulders and jostled him over to see what Milton was indicating. His guard's bruising grip only confirmed for Turner that this was one of Hetzel's half-mechanical men.

Descending from the clouds, almost silently, was a dirigible-style airship of remarkable size – four times the length of the airship *Albatross* and judging by the flags snapping in the wind made exclusively for the New Confederacy. Two balloon envelopes with the look of a mortar shell, painted a matte gray. The gondola below was a third as wide and a tenth as long as the balloon envelopes. Shaped like a shark, it didn't merely hang between the envelopes; it was directly attached to them by three huge nets of cables the size of his body that swept up and over the balloons, grasping them firmly. Sets of cables were also strung between the pair, keeping them from parting. Semi-Rigid design. Four smoke stacks jutted up from the center of the gondola at points wider than the envelopes, billowing thick black smoke. The prow of the gondola was curved and extended several feet forward from the hull before turning under and becoming the keel all the way to the aft. Windows for the Bridge were set squarely in front and likely not as well reinforced as the *Albatross's* had been. A single, giant screw whipped around its axle at the rear of the craft and two smaller propellers stabilized the vessel at the midsection.

As it approached, the sound of her engines caused the windows to vibrate. Slowly, she approached the Cliff House and finally stopped just shy of the roof. She was huge, mean, and meant to look terrifying. Her size was beyond any military or civilian airship known. The Reuters Heavy Haulers had nothing on this monster.

"Let's just say that those on the Western coast of Mexico have every intention of joining our new society. What you see might make you think we're prepared for immediate invasion, but as you say, we lack a few things. Prussia is entirely for us, but isn't ready to commit herself until we can prove our value and capacity. The same goes for Spain, though I suspect that country will never grasp the former glories it so dearly wants. Still, Spain and Prussia want back into the Americas, despite the United States' policies."

Milton saluted to some hidden ship's master, who could see all of them from the depths, and smiled.

Turner felt his stomach knot. He knew where this conversation was going. His guard remained directly behind him. Milton and the others were too comfortable with Turner's presence, meaning they weren't viewing him as threat.

This close to the Cliff House, Turner could see the machine-work that was required to create the gondola. He could see the huge plates riveted together, just as he had seen those on the *Nautilus*. If that was necessary to make Nemo's submarine water tight, then this craft was likely weather proof too. Unlike the *Nautilus*, the plates could not be iron – the ship would never lift off the ground if they were. An alloy? The same alloy that was used on the locomotive? Oh God, Willey and the military had no concept of what they were up against. A whole ship made of a metal as thick as needed to repel attack and yet the damn thing was light enough to fly.

Yet, the design was imperfect - the propellers at the midsection weren't large enough. He could see from his vantage point that the monster was struggling to maintain stability. Turner wasn't able to say how much bigger they needed to be but he knew instinctively that they were too small. The airship was barely manageable in the strong, consistent winds around the entrance to the San Francisco harbor, but should she encounter a commonly occurring Pacific typhoon, her stability would be shattered. One updraft and it might all be over. All the weight of the gondola would start to sway uncontrollably. Gale force winds catching the metal ship could drag her into a mountain; those huge balloons would act more like sails. Here, his old ship had remarkable advantages. The *Albatross* could alter which of her many screws were in use and thus create maneuverability. She could even take off almost vertically – an innovation no one had mastered yet other than Robur. It was a knowledge he wished he didn't have.

What a monster! Still, she had what a warship needed ... she had the ability to generate fear, which Tom understood.

Now he recognized why it bothered him more than should be expected: it looked like one of the Ironclads from the war. Side hatches opened and large black gun barrels rolled forward. Four guns that he could see in the clouded light. Four was more than enough to cause widespread damage. But the weight of them ... no wonder there were two gas envelopes.

Worst of all, emblazoned on its side was the vessel's name: The *NCSS Albermarle II*. Named after the ship he had sacrificed body and future to sink. Pershing had succeeded in sinking the original but lost his mind by the end of the war. It was an infamous name. Turner felt his chest tighten.

Well, this was just perfect, he thought, trying to force away the nausea that came with understanding. As if Hetzel wasn't already trying to kill him, now he had to deal with a New Confederacy. Pirates, Ghosts, Volcanoes and Mechanical Assassins. How the hell had he, a quiet man hidden in obscurity, become so broadly known and hunted by every lunatic trying to be king of the world? "And you lured me all the way out here for ...?" Turner already knew the answer but a touch of sarcasm gave him a fleeting feeling of strength.

"The tone in your voice Mister Turner tells me y'all are well aware of your value to such an enterprise as ours. You see, we have been made aware of the 'concerns' of one Monsieur Hetzel."

"It would seem Hetzel has sent telegrams and agents all over the world – one has to wonder if there is anyone who isn't aware of his concerns with me?" He indicated his guard.

"Indeed! Frankly, I think it is very foolish of him to want to kill you. Dead, y'all are of no use to anyone. Alive, y'all can share with us the designs and innovations of that madman ya'll worked for, for so long."

"I'm no engineer," Turner said flatly, well aware it might not change Milton's mind. "I believe you discovered that much for yourself?"

"No need for y'all to be. We just need your memories and

descriptions. We can take it from there – we always had our own clever men. We invented the ironclad warship and the first submarine. You Northerners simply copied and tried to keep up. No, we don't need you to be an engineer, just a receptacle of observations from which we may sample."

The guard seized Turner by the arms and Milton produced a small firearm from his coat.

Turner didn't fight. In fact, he just stood there, almost laughing. The whole thing was so absurd if not entirely improbable that he had to consider if this was a bad dream or if he had wandered into an Opium den and succumbed to its temptations?

"European funding, Prussian and Spanish professional soldiers, Mexican aristocrats fed up with their so-called democracy, and a terrified populace willing to do anything for their own safety? Add American financiers who want protections for their businesses, farmers who want water rights and the elimination of red Indians who pester them, corrupt government leadership, gold seekers who couldn't care less who's in charge, and I believe we have the perfect recipe for success."

"You just need time and proof of your commitment."

"Indeed, sir, indeed. We are on a rather tight schedule as it were. We have come to the time when we must re-introduce ourselves to the world."

Ahead of schedule, Turner realized. Ben Willey wasn't expecting this until the new year. No one was ready for this.

Pierre Jules Hetzel set aside his mundane duties, sorting through a bewildering number of poorly written submissions for publication. He took a great deal of time and effort to show the world that he was still a publisher, and such simplistic tasks gave him relief from his purpose. Occasionally, controlling the nature of books and newspapers that "informed" the masses was of invaluable assistance to his cause. So long as France was served and preserved, he was indifferent to the method.

His achievements, both behind and in front of his publishing endeavors, had been enormously successful. He printed the news as was best for the country; he encouraged the arts, and even had the pleasure of producing the works of his friends Victor Hugo and Jules Verne. Very successful indeed.

He quietly read the two telegrams handed to him by a uniformed soldier who waited at attention.

The Woman was up to something, though his agent was not able to determine what that was. A female scholar? No matter how unnatural and improbable it was, she was assuredly intelligent enough. He would have to consider if any measures might be taken against her. The thought did not sit well with him. He was a gentleman who thought she was hardly behaving as a lady – chasing around the globe, showing inappropriate interest in an *American*, lecturing in public …

All quite unseemly yet somehow intriguing. A shame really, but he could not allow a woman to disrupt his purpose.

There was one thorn in his side, one disappointment in his perfect record: Turner. The damned American simply would not die. He'd sent a number of his *improved* men and extraordinary weaponry after the wounded and friendless man, and they had failed. He'd made it back to the United States and was surviving in the deadly Barbary Coast. Any other man would have the sense to give in and pass quietly from the world, but not Turner.

Now things were threatening to explode in a political mess. He had no one to blame but himself. He'd informed a group of men calling themselves a New Confederacy that a former Union officer with specialized experience with airships was within their grasp. He had thought this would be the perfect solution to the Turner problem: bring in an old enemy with a 20 year old grudge. What he hadn't considered was the Prussian presence. Prussia, the worst enemy France had ever known in the 19th Century, might ultimately have the knowledge Turner could provide. He'd miscalculated severely and was forced to improvise. In some ways, the new plan was better than the old plan.

Dropping the telegrams from San Francisco on top of all those dreadful manuscripts, Hetzel made his decision. For France. For his beloved country.

"Contact *the Egyptian*. If Turner survives to talk of either my improved men or the advancements of his former captain, Robur, the damage might be substantial. Inform the Egyptian that, should this be the case, to act accordingly."

He sighed heavily, releasing any guilt he felt in the forced exhale. Guilt did not serve or preserve. Guilt was useless. He had acted wisely, now he would wait to react if necessary.

Slowly, Hetzel picked up another horrible submission and went about his daily business.

December 1883
NCSS Albermarle II
Pacific Coast near Point Lobos, California

Well … he had hoped to see into the interior of what was going on. *This* was not exactly what he had planned.

He had never been inside an Ironclad before, not once in his entire naval career. He'd seen the quintessential Civil War ship in dry dock and he'd stood on one – once – for a photograph. It had never been necessary for him to go belowdecks.

His guard held him tightly by the arm making the drapery cord tied around his wrists redundant. Milton's colleagues had insisted, mistakenly fearing Turner's abilities over the unknown strength of the half-mechanical guard. Turner hadn't had a chance to look at the enhanced guard very well, but he knew the glazed angry stare, the unblinking eyes, the otherwise non-descript appearance that Hetzel's creatures shared. He reached up to scratch the side of his nose, noting the reaction time and immediacy of the guard's response. A good bit of information to have.

The airship rocked severely for a matter of seconds – the storm was spilling over the coastline and into the bay. Turner took every moment to marvel at the construction of the *Albermarle II*. The gangway that led toward the gondola from the loading ramps followed along the base of the port balloon. Below him, he could see through the walkway to a lower level platform built into the rigid structure. It was as wide as the balloon at that level, and designed to carry cargo. Above him was the superstructure that held six enormous gas bags, each separated by a gap which he assumed was needed for a crewman to fit into … for repairs. At each gap, he did his best to see to the top. The interior rings were of curved metal, supported by a zigzag of struts, and reinforced with a second ring. Large pins and puzzle piece shaped cuts in the ring made him wonder if the whole thing came apart in storable pieces.

Despite the money the New Confederacy appeared to have at its disposal, they hadn't spent a penny on interior comforts. The walls were bare, unpolished metal, eliminating the weight of paint or decoration – every ounce saved was essential.

Well, I'll be damned, he thought, passing close to one of the interior rings. Bamboo and aluminum. Bamboo was cheap and plentiful, not to mention remarkably light yet strong, but aluminum was difficult to produce, unless they'd found a way to smelt it efficiently. Pipes as thick as his body ran the length of the gangway and leaked condensed steam or oils. The platform under his feet was occasionally divided into small rooms. They rattled with each stress on the whole balloon structure. The roar of an engine outside the envelope soon overwhelmed the rattling.

He knew already that there were two major innovations Captain Robur had created that could never be shared with this new abomination of a "Society": lacquered paper walls and fuel-less, self sustaining electric generators based on hydrogen. Robur had kept the *Albatross* light by eliminating heavy interior walls, limiting the use of unnecessary metal, and disregarding the concept of solid fuel, such as coal or wood. Of course, Robur's search for huge amounts of naturally produced electricity was ultimately what cost him his life. But that was the past.

They weren't using standard electrical generators such as those on their locomotive, Turner noted by the sounds that echoed throughout the whole ship and the glow of chemical non-electric lighting, yet the technology was certainly available. Robur hadn't originated the idea; he'd simply mastered it beyond anyone else's comprehension: he generated power with limited use of heavy fuel. He illuminated the whole interior of the *Albatross* with electric light. Hell, even Nemo used such power for his *Nautilus*. But not here.

Hydrogen was the key. Turner would die before telling them; this much he accepted. The trick now was to avoid being interrogated on that particular subject.

The ship vibrated more at the midsection. The engines must be located there, he decided. They hadn't calibrated the angles of their screws, and they were causing heavy cavitations against the air. She was not silent by any stretch of the imagination, but the sound would likely reach a battlefield too late for anyone to identify what it was and react fully. Good God, there was something else he knew that he couldn't tell them.

Urgency. Milton had said it; the New Confederacy had to

prove itself as soon as it could. Prussia couldn't afford to keep pouring good money into a bad deal. That would make the *Albermarle II* more important than the locomotive – it was armed and in flight, even with old fashioned engines.

The gangway turned to a stairway, allowing Turner a view of the *Albermarle's* gondola as they descended. Across the roof of the gondola, the only truly solid structure, were rail tracks made from carved channels in the flooring, but the locomotive was not there. The airship was built to carry it anywhere it needed to go. A flying warship indeed, as well as a transport. And his next guess was that the gondola could be carried by the locomotive along with her deflated gas sacks. Such a plan would work if the rigid frames collapsed into a transportable size. A reciprocal arrangement seemed likely. The operation would not be limited by existing rail lines, geography, or oceanic conditions – all elements that would slow down a Federal response to the threat both vehicles represented.

Before entering the gondola, he noted the flexibility of the cable mounts. The damn thing could utilize one or both balloons.

How the hell had they built this thing without anyone noticing? And where?

As he entered the Bridge, his guard's grip still pinching his upper arm, he finally, fully accepted that this was no longer an experiment in wishful thinking for Milton and his men – staring down at the roof of the Cliff House and a gathering of around one hundred men on the beach – noting the presence of Prussian, Spanish, and old Confederate uniforms all around him – this was all too real.

Milton waved over a man in a black wool uniform with a surprising lack of gold braid or shining medals. Older than Milton by a decade, the officer almost floated over to them, his movements unimpressed and dignified. His shoulders were set straight enough to satisfy any measurement by a square and he held his chin aloft on an iron bar of a neck surrounded by a tall black collar. Two hands taller than Turner, he dominated the room. Others were covered in their pompous assumptions of wealth, swirling in gold braids, embroidery, and polish, but this man was clearly the man in charge.

Blonde and gray hair mixed; eyes as intensely blue as Turner's; and an impressive moustache, thick and broad with only the ends neatly waxed. Draped along the length of his chin was a beard that uniformly curved under, defining his jaw. He appeared chiseled from cold marble.

"Admiral Hagen, I should like to introduce ya'll to Mister Turner." The Admiral gave a sharp nod. Milton didn't bother with the second part of a formal greeting, knowing he didn't need Turner's permission to be introduced to the Admiral. "Mister Turner is here to assist us in improving the performance of this here aircraft. I, myself, have ..."

Hagen moved closer to Turner, effectively cutting off Milton. He stared at Milton's prisoner for a minute before lifting his chin and speaking. "Mr. Turner, let us dispense with the pleasantries." His voice was deep, damaged, and slightly accented. His English was exact. "You were the subordinate of a man who called himself Robur. You served on an airship that foolishly allowed itself to be seen by a crowd of people, some of whom had the intelligence to take note of some of her innovations. Naturally, no one saw the ship long enough to be precise. That is why you are allowed to be here. We otherwise have no use for spies or saboteurs."

"Sir. I expected as much." Turner did his best to relax his shoulders. He was not afraid of Milton but this man elicited another reaction – something far more primitive. "If we are dispensing with pleasant chat, then allow me to tell you that I was not an engineer or designer on Captain Robur's ship. I steered her ..."

The Admiral's eyebrow raised.

"... and I ran errands for my captain. Robur kept such creations of his mind to himself."

"And yet, you steered her. You knew your ship, how she handled, why she handled the way she did. Are you telling me you never repaired her?"

This was getting worse, as if it could. "Repairs were directed by the captain." Not entirely true, but enough so. "I am not in the habit of speaking ill of the dead, and he was my captain whom I'll consider with respect always," he was relieved as he noted the Admiral's expression alter slightly. "Yet the truth of the matter is, Captain Robur was in the end paranoid, secretive, and likely insane. He shared nothing with me."

At first, Hagen didn't move. Milton wisely kept back but watched. Some of the other officers well behind them mumbled and noticed, but did nothing to indicate they would have a reaction until Hagen chose to have one. Slowly, the sides of the blonde moustache rose. "I must confess I had not thought you would be so loyal. It is refreshing. It is, however, regrettable that he is not here to return the favor to you. And we, with the same regret, must not take your word for it all. I'm afraid that if you will not or cannot answer my questions fully and satisfactorily, then we must ask them differently."

The ship jolted sharply, the storm now hurling its pent up energy in increasing winds. Hagen and Turner, old sailors, their bodies trained by years of shipboard life, adjusted to the swaying without consciously doing so.

Turner waited, expecting some sort of stabilizing equipment to take over. Nothing. That would be Hagen's primary interest. Turner forced his expression to remain as calm as possible. The fists he kept together were so tight his fingers were losing feeling. Panic would only get him killed. "I have given you context for any answer you want. The truth is that I know little to nothing of the actual engineering of the *Albatross*."

"I find that difficult to believe, though I will allow that you might believe so yourself."

Milton smiled. "As I told you Admiral he's a Federal man all the way. Even if he did know about the designs and inventions, he wouldn't want to share them, now would you Turner?" Suddenly, Milton produced his small pistol and pointed it at Turner's forehead.

A bark of laughter slipped past Turner's lips. "Are you telling me I have a choice between dying before telling you something I might accidentally know or after being tortured? Go ahead. Shoot."

Both men were amazed when the Admiral reached over, grasped Milton by the wrist, and forcibly lowered his hand. "You of all men must understand that this is the business of war and it is not personal."

"A New Confederacy, on American soil, with foreign assistance? I take that very personally, sir. That you intend to force me to provide a means to risk my country's safety and future, that too, sir, I take personally."

Milton sneered. "Well, aren't you just the perfect patriot?"

"You, sir, can go to hell if you aren't already on your way. Milton, you're a lap dog to better men who will help you take over parts of two countries then yank the rug from under your feet. Do you really think a country that has been trying to regain its former glories before it's swallowed up by the German States will toss you money and wish you luck? Do you really believe Spanish interests will be fulfilled by handing control of Mexico and Baja to you?"

It was Hagen who spoke while Milton opened his mouth. "Turner, you are partially correct. We will have an active presence in the New Confederacy, but for less obvious reasons. The last time we invested in a Confederacy, they lost. Therefore, we lost. It is not our intention to repeat this. Your country, Turner, needs to accept that the ... what do you call it ... land grab in the West it conducted was too much too soon. The reconstruction of the South was badly done and those people will always be in a state of hatred and rebellion unless they have a place of their own. We in Prussia we are facing something akin to your situation and for the sake of our people need to establish a strong presence in this region, Africa, and the Indies."

"I wouldn't recommend the Indies at the moment, unless you are fond of burying bodies and shoveling volcanic ash."

Hagen nodded considerately. "It will be some time before the Indies recovers from the disaster you witnessed. We both suspect the same thing, yes? That the local tribesmen and villagers have had enough of the Dutch and will force them out. At that time, they too will need funding, leadership, and organization. Many say things about us, but we Prussians are renowned for our discipline and organization."

"And your ambition."

"Indeed."

"Not to mention ruthlessness?"

Hagen seemed amused. "You should ask the French about that."

December 1883
Fort Winfield Scott
(popularly known as Fort Point)
Entrance to the San Francisco Bay

The Commandant of the Fort stood with his hat dripping wet from the rain, his coat flapping in the growing wind, and his coffee cup halfway to his lips. He'd seen the "Monitors," the Ironclads, before. He'd seen them in the waters of the Mississippi River, patrolling after the taking of Vicksburg and New Orleans. He'd seen them in the Gulf of Mexico. But, always from the vantage of looking directly across or slightly from above those ships. He was staring now at the keel of one. Held above his Fort by gigantic balloons and flying what appeared to be the Confederate flag, he knew what it was by its grotesque design and heavily armored exterior. A flying Ironclad, descending from the clouds like the wrath of God.

After allowing too much time to pass in disbelief, he noted the look of shock on his Lieutenant, and the astonished stare of a naval Commander who'd come to see him. To warn him.

He wasn't hallucinating. The Commandant called out, demanding immediate action.

There was no possible way to turn their guns toward the airship. Hell, no one knew the damn things could fly. Except of course the naval Commander at his side. The young man had come to the Fort to warn of odd vessels, trains, and potential threats. To his credit, the naval man didn't panic.

"We never planned for *this*."

"What did you say, Willey?"

"This is bigger than we imagined. Where the hell is Turner?"
Yes, where the hell are you Tom Turner, he thought. Why aren't you here, telling us what this thing is and how to beat it?

As he was backed into, one of the seven support poles that held up the canopy over the Bridge, Turner took notice of every man he could see. While his original plan to simply gather information had gone awry, he was not without options, he kept telling himself. Milton was determined but caught up in his fantasy about the rise of a New Confederate nation. That would mean he was unwilling to accept reality. He was ultimately weak, though in terms of a fast response, Milton could be deadly. With Milton were four other New Confederates, each more likely to protect his waistcoat than his own skin, and certainly not someone else's. Only one was armed that Turner could tell: Milton. Of course Hagen was armed, if not practically, then ceremonially. Then of course, there was the half-mechanical guard who pinioned him effectively while one of his wrists was unbound to allow his arms to be pulled behind him.

"Forgive our rudeness, Mr. Turner," the Admiral said as he scanned the fort below him, "but I would prefer you to remain out of the way."

Milton pulled away Turner's long cravat while the guard held his arms behind the support pole. The Confederate took his sweet time, conspicuously admiring Turner's scar as the handiwork of one of his rebellious colleagues. Christ, while he distrusted Southerners, he hated Milton and his unfounded cockiness most of all.

A moment later, the guard was re-binding Turner's wrists together behind him, while Milton held him in place by his throat. Turner ground his teeth together, forcing his expression to be neutral – non-threatening – the exact opposite of the storm churning in his gut and putting violent ideas in his head. He could withstand much, but something beyond a shirt collar touching his throat sent his mind wildly into chaotic mixes of fear, hate, and aggression. Hold on, give him nothing, he thought with all his life. He had to wait. This was not the right time to move.

He then struggled for a moment, protesting obviously … distractingly. Loudly he demanded if Milton knew that *this* was not how a prisoner of war was treated? Had he learned nothing from the war? Turner's efforts were dismissed as unnecessary – he was trapped on the airship – and the usual admonishments were made.

Typical, Turner thought as he felt the guard finish the bonds with a sharp tug. In his right hand, he'd caught some of the length of the drapery cord during his distracting protestations. He managed to gather some slack which, and if the Turner Luck would hold out a little longer, he could then release from between his fingers, loosening what should have been a tight binding. But not yet.

Turner stood perfectly still, wondering what the Admiral was planning. Hagen was his chief worry. The Admiral was formidable but practical. He wore a polished, formal sidearm which Turner had no doubt he would use. Two high ranking men had the look of Spaniards in their green and gold tunics. Six more men, Prussian by uniform, were at the controls of the airship and exceptionally focused on their work. The airship was so ungainly that Turner had concluded she required a full troop of men just to keep her afloat. Compared to the *Albatross*, the *Albermarle* was ungainly and clumsy.

There was the terror factor that the *Albermarle* could achieve, which Robur had never intended for his airship. For a few moments, while the Admiral was giving orders, Turner considered the effect this behemoth had on those who could observe its approach and carrion-like hover over them. It would be a fearful thing to see.

Milton broke his thoughts by grabbing his collar, tugging, and pulling his shirt open to reveal the scar even more. "It would seem, Mister Turner, we didn't' do our job very well. I can assure you that should you fail to cooperate, I'll make certain that you hang proper this time. Perhaps you should not be so eager to die for your country."

Of the threats Turner had laughed off or dismissed, there was one that easily made its way through the layers of experienced survival, honed defenses, and damned good luck to pierce his soul: a return to the moment which should have claimed his life. To that feeling of suspension and desperation, the struggle for breath, the sickening choking sounds ...

It had to have shown in Turner's expression for Milton smiled. His eyes glanced at Turner's pocket. He looked surprised for a moment. Opening Turner's coat, he touched the leather journal.

Lettie's letter was inside.

Milton could never know about her.

"A man might wonder about a fellow who likes looking and

touching another man too much," Turner blurted out, hoping the vulgar suggestion would offend the sensibilities of a self-proclaimed gentleman like Milton.

Milton stepped back and produced his gun again. His grip on it wasn't strong and Turner knew he'd said exactly the right thing to make him leave off the examination of his personal belongings.

"Mr. Milton," the Admiral said, without turning to look at the man, "I believe we should allow Mr. Turner an unimpeded view of the proceedings. You will need to remove yourself to a more advantageous place."

Glaring at the Prussian, Milton wasn't sure just how to take that. "Why?"

"Because I would like Mr. Turner to understand what is at stake here." With the slowness of a confident killer, Hagen brought himself over to Turner at his leisure, unshaken by what he knew he'd say. "I'm quite certain you will give your life for your country, perhaps even for the madman you once served even though he is long dead. I confess I admire that. But I have no use for it. You are, like many, weakened by the idea of innocence." He put out his arm and prodded the Confederate away – never once looking at him. "I do not, myself, consider a professional soldier an innocent, but there are times when he is not in battle or unaware that you have declared war on him."

Behind Hagen, Turner could see the strangely shaped, thick masonry of Fort Point at the base of the cliffs, near the Presidio. Surely if he could see the Fort, then the military units bivouacked there would be able to see the *Albermarle*? And, Turner knew, it would be a fearful thing.

"Mr. Turner. We have been preparing for some time. Vessels such as this are not made quickly. We have been planning on how best to use our strategic first strike on the United States. The Fort below is hardly a vital target as it has only two hundred men, small scale artillery, and is but one vantage point from which to defend the San Francisco bay. It has, however, propaganda merit. It is prominent, it *is* a military installation, and it is famous. Presidents have gone there. Your Lincoln did not, but General Grant did after he became a President. Despite its limits, the people of this region regard it as an important monument. To me, this makes it a target of note."

Nodding, as though violently compelled to agree with Hagen's assessment, Turner replied, "And you'll attack it if what? If I don't give you engineering secrets I swear to God above I do not have? Two hundred men's lives?" His eyes grew wide and he strained forward. He had not thought they were ready to make such an aggressive move. Why had they moved up their timetable?

Hagen's expression never changed from disengaged, unaffected. "Yes. Look at what it takes to keep the *Albermarle* aloft. Anything you could offer to make this vessel more efficient is worth any cost. Can we not now discuss what you do and do not know?"

Turner's mouth was brutally dry. He couldn't move without being shot and he could do little to help the Ft. Point men if he was dead. "I am telling you I do not know anything."

It was Milton's voice that shattered the brittle air around them. "We need to make our stand now; to make a statement that the New Confederacy is a factor in the world at large. We are no longer in the shadows waiting for glory days to come – they are here."

The Admiral continued to ignore Milton, which was beginning to create its own atmosphere of tension. "Mr. Turner. I appeal to your sense of duty."

"You're going to kill them anyway," he said after a very long, thoughtful moment. It wasn't the Admiral who'd given away the plans, it was the idiot Milton. He knew not to smile at his discovery or how it had been worth his life to learn it, if only he could make use of his presence. "Milton just played your hand for you, sir. You are launching your New Order, your New Utopia, not later but here and now. Any words on my part will not stop you. You've already started this war." When Hagen opened his mouth to interrupt, Turner raised his voice. "You selected the target, revealed yourself, and now you're here to do your worst. I'm a surprise – a bonus – but not the reason for your presence. No matter what I say, you are going to attack."

For a moment, Hagen's expression brightened. He was tired of the grandstanding and noise-making Confederate. There were plenty of clever men amongst the new Confederacy: clever men who knew better than to be on the airship during the first attack. This man, Turner, was a relief from Milton's lack of experience and knowledge. What a shame.

He decided to say nothing. He turned away and strode up to the center of the Bridge.

"I should like to say a few words, Admiral ..."

Hagen's hand snapped up and silenced Milton with the gesture. "Wars do not start with speeches. They are continued with them. They are ended with them. But never started." He gave a direct nod to a man waiting behind a large targeting scope. "Align guns." His clipped Prussian added a sharp edge to such a simple statement. The command was repeated twice by descending ranked officers, and the third time it was shouted into a communication tube, presumably connected to the gunnery.

The gun ports had been opened and now her huge guns were rolled out. The grinding noise of the operation shook the whole ship.

"Admiral. Stop. This isn't an act of war, it's murder." He let the slack of rope go from his fingers and began twisting his hands, trying to free them, attempting to mask the obvious exertion. "This goes against every convention of honorable combat."

"No, Mr. Turner. It is a surprise attack. That is often the first action of offense one makes."

"They don't know they are at war. No conflict has been declared. Surely that does not sit well with you?" He kept straining his hands, but his bindings wouldn't loosen. He had to do something.

"Open fire," he commanded, with icy composure.

The ship jerked violently as each volley was fired. The roar of the guns was nearly deafening, even on the protected Bridge. The airship began to falter with each succeeding blast and no fewer than four men had to fight her controls to keep her relatively steady.

It's a damn flying coffin, Turner realized. And we're killing everyone below. He pulled until he was sure his flesh was tearing – but his hands wouldn't come free. The cord had caught on itself. He had to do something – anything.

Below, the members of three bivouacked units did their best to turn their defenses to an enemy descending from the sky. It was a nightmare none had thought of. Balloons had been used in war before, but not this size, not this scale ...

The forward rampart burst into splinters of rock and flame,

killing every man within ten feet of it. The hole left in the deep walls looked like an impact crater. Shell after shell dropped onto their heads and exploded at their feet.

Willey stepped back, trying to gain a view of the situation which might suggest a response. The soldier next to him staggered forward, soaked in his own blood, and fell to the floor. Snagging up the man's Spenser, Willey began firing at the huge ship. First he aimed for the open ports, in the hopes of hitting a gunner. Then at the narrow windows, in a blind attempt at hitting someone on the Bridge. Then at the biggest targets, though it was mostly hidden behind the body of the vessel: the balloon envelopes.

The firing stopped. Willey counted six volleys. Now they were reloading? Or just waiting to see what damage they had inflicted before adding more injury.

"Sir, if we can ..." he started to say.

The Commandant was arched backward over the rampart, coffee cup still in his locked grip, missing portions of his body from the collarbone up. A shell had hit and mutilated him instantly. Less than two feet from Willey. The naval Commander tried not to heave his guts onto the floor. Clerking in Washington had never given him the skills to face such destruction.

"Commander?" The Lieutenant looked over at him, clearly no better prepared for such wanton death.

Think, think, think! "See the gas bags?" Willey pointed upwards, his fingers soaked immediately by the rain. "Find a gun, any gun: a rock, if that's all we have. Turn it around and aim up! That has to be filled with helium."

"It's ... it's just a ..."

"Not just a balloon. They've protected it from their own smoke stacks. They don't want sparks near it. They don't want fire, but we'll give it to them." He was guessing. It was all that they had. "Move man! Before they reload and start firing again."

"What will you trade, Mr. Turner?"

No reply came to Turner's lips. He could see what a few shells had done. Perhaps it was that they were falling and thus increasing in their speed. Or a new type of shell. Or just damn lucky. Six volleys, and the Fort was on fire. How many men had died? He hadn't stopped it. He couldn't have, but that offered no comfort.

"I will consider this enough for now. A signal to your government that a war has begun. But you, Mr. Turner, can make the decision as to whether we stay and bombard the Fort again, or leave now as the victors."

Milton stepped between them. "Admiral, I will not be ignored anymore. See here, we came here to eliminate an enemy and we are staying to the end. To the end of that there Fort. If we leave now, they'll reckon that we are weak."

"Quite the contrary, Mr. Milton. They will have no idea what we are capable of and will naturally underestimate us. However, I am willing to remain – to fire again. Mr. Turner, the decision is yours."

All eyes focused on Turner, who couldn't take his eyes off of the burning Fort below him. He had to do something – anything!

"Mr. Turner, do you know how to stabilize a ship of this size? As you may have noticed, stability is not our strength."

Slowly Turner nodded. Yes, he did know that much about airship design.

"Excellent. Tell me how Robur accomplished it." As Turner glared back, refusing to speak, Hagen became visibly frustrated for the first time. "There is no sense in keeping this to yourself. Tell me how to stabilize this ship."

Milton clenched his fists and walked up behind the Admiral, who continued ignoring him. "Admiral, you are to resume hostilities."

"As I said, sir. You are going to kill those men anyway." Turner glared at them both.

"No longer, Mr. Turner. We have made our statement. Now, I have the option to fly away."

"Then, I … I will give you what I can. I didn't lie to you before: I am not an engineer. If you leave this battle now, on my honor, I will tell you what I know." He meant it. His cleverness had failed. His hands would not be freed and he could only stop the bombardment with a promise.

"It has been a pleasure, Mr. Turner, to deal with a man whose honor is genuine. You remain loyal to Robur, though the man is dead and was, as you said, insane. You stand by your country even though you were abandoned by them. I will accept your word." If for the briefest moment, an expression of admiration swept across Hagen's face. "Turn her about and return to the Cliff House."

A hand clamped down on the Admiral's shoulder and spun him around. Milton's fist slammed into his face. Hagen dropped to the deck, dazed. Men from the New Confederacy drew weapons, most of which were Bowie knives. In seconds, the Spanish officers were at the mercy of the Confederates, as were the Prussian crewmen. Turner's guard remained silent, nonreactive, freakishly still.

"We will not withdraw like cowards. You! Boy! Call down to the gunnery and order them to start firing again. They're not to stop till I order them to stop!"

The Prussian looked to his Admiral, who was dusting himself off with annoyance.

"Ah said, order them to shoot!"

The Prussian turned to the communications tube.

Turner cried out, straining against the pole, "No. I'll tell you what I know! I'll stabilize your ship. Don't fire."

"A little too late, Mister Turner. Much too late."

Turner pulled on the rope one more time. This time, it was enough for him to twist his hands and slide one wrist out, while the Admiral called over to his officer in German to stand where he was, to refuse Milton's command. Milton was too busy managing Hagen and the young officer to care about Turner's struggles.

Milton stomped over to the officer, grasped the man by the hair and pushed his gun under the man's jaw. "Now, you Prussians are going to have to understand a few things. This is the New Confederacy, not the new Prussia. We are in command. It is our country – our legacy – our future."

Turner leapt forward, shouldering the Admiral out of his way, flinging his body into the ship's wheel. The crewman manning it had no time to react and landed sprawling on the deck. The wheel began spinning uncontrollably to port – toward the ocean side of the Presidio and the Golden Gate – away from Fort Point. Officers and crewmen, and the half-mechanical guard, grasped anything they could for stability as the ship careened away from the burning Fort. Turner reached up to the gear shaft that controlled elevation. His hand gripped the release clamp.

Hagen's hands wrapped around Turner's face and throat, yanking him backward. As the ship dropped several meters to port, both men slid around the gear shafts. Hagen climbed on top of Turner, wrapped his arm around his neck and squeezed.

Milton cursed and charged at both men, falling over the Admiral, effectively freeing Turner. A mistake. Turner was on his feet, gripped the control shaft, and pointed the *Albermarle* down toward the water. The airship was not designed for such a maneuver and after falling a hundred feet, righted itself, yet kept descending. Pacific winds battered the gondola, causing it to sway.

As Milton got onto his feet, Turner's fist pounded his nose, his mouth, his nose again. The pistol dropped to the floor.

A knife came up under his chin. It wasn't a Bowie knife: it was an elegant officer's dagger. The Admiral held him in place but didn't seem too troubled by the damage Turner had inflicted on Milton. His concern was the uncontrolled descent of his airship.

To Hetzel's half-mechanical guard, he shouted, "Level the ship before we crash." He gulped in a mouthful of air and squared his shoulders, never moving the sharp blade away from Turner. "Mr. Turner, I would be more than happy to allow you to kill Milton, but I may have need of him later. You and I, instead, will discuss this ship. I have your word. You gave it to me."

"Under the promise that you would withdraw from Fort Point. You didn't, I did that for you."

"An unnecessary gesture as my men would have regained control of the ship." He turned his attention briefly to the guard. "You – take the wheel – now!" He adjusted the blade slightly. "You see, I would have control again."

"Before or after you shelled the Fort a second time? Answer me that, sir."

Hagen grunted an approval. "I believe before. As my intention was honorable, I expect that you will react honorably yourself." He swallowed another gulp of air. "Stand up, Mr. Turner, or I will cut your throat and go back to the Fort to finish destroying it."

"You hide well behind the lives of other men." Turner practically spit it out.

"A time honored tradition. You break easily when confronted

with the extinction of said men. We all operate for the best of our hopes. For you and me, it is our country. For men like Milton, it is a dream of glory long past."

A terrified gasp came out of the mouths of nearly every man on the Bridge.

One of the disarmed Confederates shouted first. "God in Heaven, we're crashing."

The *Albermarle* had sunk below the elevation of the Headlands cliffs, near one of the Coastal Batteries and was being blown by high winds into the twisted, tilted, exposed basalt.

"What are you doing!" The Admiral stood up, watching in horror as Turner's guard held a death grip on the wheel; locked into a destructive course.

"He won't answer you," Turner called up to the Prussian, "not all of them can speak."

"All of who or what? Milton! What did you bring aboard my ship?"

The thought had not occurred to him. Turner suddenly knew what was happening. Pierre Jules Hetzel, French patriot and ardent Franco-Republican, would never allow the Prussians to create such a deadly weapon. "Admiral, he was never sent to guard me. He was sent to board your ship and protect the future of France. Don't you understand that?"

The Admiral stared, his face burning red. His ship was being sabotaged. He reached down and sized Turner by the collar, pointing the dagger at his face. "Who sent him!"

"Hetzel. Pierre Hetzel the ..." Turner didn't finish his sentence before Hagen knew exactly what was being said.

Aiming all his fury at Milton, "A goddamned French saboteur. You brought an agent of our enemy on to this ship. Onto my ship!"

Hagen's face, for the first time, showed panic. His ship ... *His* ship! The *Albermarle II* was crashing indeed and Hetzel's half-mechanical man was steering her directly into destruction.

The cliffs of the Headlands leading out to Point Bonita Lighthouse were colorful, jagged, slanted awkwardly, and approaching so quickly that Turner assumed the worst – the airship would shatter against those cliffs, crashing down into to the rocks and sea below.

Hagen let go of Turner, running toward the enhanced guard. The half-mechanical man held onto the wheel, uncaring that he too would die with the crew. Two Prussian crewmen yanked at his arms; pounded his head with anything they could grab. The guard held his course.

His ship would not be destroyed by a French-created monstrosity. Hagen waited for the guard to be distracted, stepped behind him, and cut through the flesh of the man's throat. Shaking at first, the guard dropped to the deck, at last relieved of his unnatural life.

That was simply done, Hagen thought, feeling his nerves release. His next orders were sharp and clear: arrest Milton and regain control of the ship.

Too late.

The *Albermarle* smashed her starboard side into the cliffs, recoiling violently as the balloon envelope floundered in ocean gales that kept the craft careening into the rock face. Glass sprayed across the Bridge as she pounded again and again into the Headlands cliff. Shards spun across the floor or flew as shrapnel.

It was the airship's iron plating that kept her from becoming an elevated shipwreck. Yet, as she struck her side again, even the rivets jarred loose and the whole ship's design began to fail. The groaning from the metal was overwhelmed by the screeching of metal on rock as the ship was dragged up the cliff face by the gales. One of the giant nets slung around the starboard balloon twisted precariously.

Winds grabbed at the sagging envelopes and her remaining

support structure, dragging the whole up and over the top of the tallest cliff, toppling the great Ironclad gondola onto her side. A giant gouged trench was left behind as the winds pulled the structure further across the hilltop and finally left it for dead.

Quiet beyond the groaning metal and wind whipping through tall redwood trees, lingered for many moments. The starboard balloon sank slowly, deflating at least two or three of its torn bags. Splintered bamboo and twisted aluminum rocked in the drafts blowing across the ground. The mighty had indeed fallen, taking a portion of the hilltop forest with her.

Much of the crew abandoned the wreckage without a word, crawling or limping away from the remains of the ship and many comrades. Tom lay quietly counting every bruise and the remarkable lack of broken bones. That damn Turner luck. His feet moved. His fingers moved. And slowly, his whole body moved. His life had been saved by that damn Turner luck and a heavy, wooden table which held his left leg pinned but otherwise undamaged. His lip was bleeding and every muscle ached in a searing, throbbing pain, but he was alive. One had to be alive to feel that much pain.

Milton lay no more than three feet from him, still clutching his pistol. By the impossible angle of his head, it was obvious that Milton would never rise again with his beloved New Confederacy. Next to him, piled in an undignified crumple, was the half-mechanical guard's body. Hagen was nearest the *Albermarle's* wheel and seemed to have survived.

Kicking at the table, Turner managed to free himself. Well, he'd been wrong. While not broken, his leg was cut and with the pressure of the table removed, it stung and bled.

The ship groaned as the winds picked up again. The hurricane force gales shifted the big airship, and both Turner and Hagen braced themselves for another crash. Slowly, the port envelope lifted then settled down again.

"So … she wants to fly." Hagen said with a freakish chuckle, trying to catch his breath and not to laugh at the same time. The twist in his left leg would keep him lying still for the immediate moment if not disabled over time. "This cannot make you very happy, Mr. Turner."

"*You* are still alive. That does not make me very happy, Admiral." He was a toothless lion, snarling over a dead carcass with another injured beast. "At least this thing won't murder any more soldiers, from any country."

Hagen nodded, oddly enough. He merely turned his head as a burst of wind knocked a chunk of bamboo off the structure and in his direction. It fell short of him with a dull thump. "I think I will not credit Mr. Milton after all, for being aware of the threat posed by the … what did you call it?"

"Hetzel calls them 'improved.'"

"Milton thought he had a new ally. One who sent him presents and gave him respect, yes?"

Turner bit at his inner lip as he pulled himself away from the table. "He thought he had a prize. A new toy to play with. And admiration for his twisted notion of bringing plantation life back to my country. Just another son of a bitch Dixie slaver …"

Hagen lay quietly, thinking how certain he was that Turner would not drag himself over to shoot him, or worse. He understood Turner perhaps better than Turner did. "You are too harsh, Mr. Turner. Your hatred for the South clouds your judgment. You falsely reduce everyone to either good or bad, but this misleads you. Not every creature from your southern states is evil or threatening, any more than any man from elsewhere. There are only two categories of men: masters and servants. I have decided which one you are."

Such an idea frightened Turner more than any injury he'd suffered – and Hagen could see through him so easily and coldly, to comprehend his prejudice better than Turner did. The comments flung his thoughts into a chaos he had hoped to avoid: thoughts any good man after a war must consider. Hagen was right about his unfair judgment of Southerners: Turner had falsely concluded that Milton and his cohorts were bad men only because of their birth and manner of speech. He had been correct in his assessment of the danger but had based it on the wrong assumptions.

"I will give to you a simple piece of advice," Hagen began, slowing rolling onto his side, completely unafraid of Turner. "Forget your past and disbelieve in viable innocence. Good versus evil: useless. Life is war and humans fight by nature. Only the masters of conflict shall be victors. All others are meant to serve. Love, peace, and innocence are falsehoods invented by those who resist their place under their masters. It has little to nothing to do with religions or philosophies. It is a simple matter of truth." At last he looked directly at Turner. "You are one who should be a master. Honor is the only thing of value to men like us. All else is meant to distract you from your rightful place. This, your old enemy the South took for granted; that their lineage or money entitled them. Most know better now, that mastery is hard fought for, maintained through strength and honor. And war. It is given to none. Even he who is a master by nature cannot become one without conflict. Abandon the frailties of preconception and you will cease to be limited by your past."

"Why tell me this?"

"Perhaps I see something of my own missteps in you. Perhaps I appreciate a true, honorable warrior, seeing them so infrequently in these modern times."

The very thought that he shared a single similarity with Hagen made him sick. Turner stood up at last, and began to limp away. He didn't want Hagen to be right about anything, let alone his continuing rage at the South. As for masters and slaves, well, there was no argument Hagen could make that would convince him of that philosophy. But Turner did need to stop thinking in terms of pre-established good and bad. Now his head hurt.

"You are still frail, Mr. Turner. You cannot leave me alive."

Turner waited by the only safe exit in the gondola.

Hagen rolled onto his back again, grinding his teeth in pain. His leg was likely ruined. "This ship was designed to fly with only her most minimal parts intact. This we designed correctly. I have the means to inflate one of the balloons, to right the gondola, to fly away. And I will."

"Do you want to die, Admiral?"

"No, of course not. But a master of warfare cannot leave me alive. Perhaps I like the idea of dying for my country and knowing I have been replaced by someone who could, if unfettered by nonsense, be a greater master of war than me. If one must die, it is a satisfying thought."

For a long time, Turner listened to the wind, his mind filling in the sound of the gun shot. The noise was hideous but he could bring himself to be its cause. Hagen ought to die for those he'd killed – but it had been war. What laws could be applied to only one soldier but not all? Henry Wirz, the prison commandant, had been executed for his role in the war, but why not Turner? Had he not killed other men? Wouldn't Hagen be easily dispatched?

All those years of fighting to end fighting: could he have been wrong? The decade spent with Robur, hopeful that the inventor would design the means to end war, now look how that had ended. Night after night of haunted dreams, of battles lost, of hopelessness.

The leather journal, weighing heavily in his pocket, held his hope. *Her letter.* His proof. Proof that there was indeed hope, if small and relatively insignificant in a world of generals, assassins, and yes … evil men.

Hagen was wrong.

Any creature could kill and could do so by nature. He was not anyone and there was one woman out there who believed there was more to him. Albert Forrer, Commander Ehrlich, even the new King of Hawai'i believed it. Who was he to disagree?

"Where do you go, Mr. Turner?"

"Far away from you and your twisted logic. You get to live today, Admiral, because you are right about one thing: the world is not filled with only good and evil. Some of us are just plain confused, hopeful, maybe a little stupid or naïve, and definitely frail. Go be Master of the World – I don't care. But like every man who ever thought he was worthy of the title, you'll fail if you haven't already."

Turner stared out through the torn opening in the Bridge at a pair of huge crows, sitting in a redwood tree, seeming to laugh at the whole wreckage. The *Albermarle II* would never fly again and the crows knew it, he was sure. Still, it would be wise to let Willey know as soon as possible and to have him glean whatever knowledge his friend could from the wreckage.

December 1883
The Asian Pacific and Southern Airship, Railroad, and Overland Wagon Company, San Francisco, California

This time, it was Turner who stepped out of the rain soaked shadows to meet with a man who'd summoned him. He looked like hell.

Willey looked officious and annoyed. "You knew they would clean out the warehouse, didn't you? Tell me at least that much. But if you did, why in God's name didn't you get us word sooner?"

"Of course they emptied the place. See here, Willey, I sent you word as fast as I could, but they haven't laid a Tipsy Line across the Gate and I had to find a telegraph office in Sausalito to get you word." As Willey ran his hands through his hair, getting angrier by the minute, Turner waited, watching. "Is anything left? Anything at all?"

"Not a pin or stick." Willey held up a message he'd received seconds before. "Your hilltop looks like a battlefield of broken machinery, but no actual airship. Pieces, but the main vessel is gone. You warned us." He sighed heavily then looked at Turner with a small spark of humor in his eyes. "And I'm never going to get a look at that damned locomotive, am I?"

"If the color and silence built into its design is an indication, you're not supposed to get a look at it." Willey's eyes grew so big he was afraid his friend might have some sort of seizure. "I have plenty to tell you of that. And I will. Not sure you'll believe me, but ..."

"Goddamn it!" He struck his leg with his hat and contemplated punching his fist through the wall. "Alright, Turner. Out with it – all of it. Including your decision to get caught up in all this, but not tell me a damn thing! You told me you were leaving town."

Turner shrugged. "I thought I was, but as you said, it's my country."

"Fine time to rediscover your patriotic nature!"

"No need to rediscover anything, it was right with me all the time. Always has been, even if I showed it a mite oddly. The last thing I wanted was to endanger good people, but this I couldn't ignore."

"From the top then." Willey folded his arms.

"No drink? I at least offered *you* a drink."

Willey didn't move or comment.

"You're going to need one. This story gets more queer by the minute. Let me do this chronologically – it's the only way it will make sense. I promise the climax of the story is the flying Ironclad. And yes, before you ask, I did get names."

Willey looked more or less like his head was going to explode. "Shall I leave off the ghosts?"

"I'd appreciate it if you would." Willey's face looked exhausted but he didn't move.

"I'll tell you another time."

The naval man opened his mouth to speak, but was interrupted by a seaman who saluted smartly and waved them both over. "Sir, we've found something."

Willey held up a hand, stared at Turner, but replied to the seaman, "We'll be there in a moment." After the fellow saluted again, Willey leaned in. "You've always been a good storyteller. Comes with the job of spies and intelligencers. Finish the damn story."

What was left? The Barbary Coast, the Palace Hotel, hiding in the slum hotel. Then he got to the good stuff. The New Confederacy, the locomotive, Milton, Prussians, and the *Albermarle II*. The last, with all the detail Turner could provide, left Willey with his jaw slack. "They're serious about snatching the whole West coast? With a flying warship and a nearly invisible locomotive? Good Christ."

"I have a theory, if you're interested."

"Let's hear it."

Turner set his hand on Willey's shoulder. "Ben, that airship was only miraculously in the air. Chances are, it was expensive to build and I can tell you it was a horror to fly. That's why they wanted me. Word has spread about my days with Robur, and as the sole survivor of the *Albatross*, I possess an understanding of her basic operations."

Looking up, he grasped Turner's wrist. "You *can* tell us what kept Robur's ship in the air."

"I don't believe so. Damn it, Ben, I'm no engineer."

Willey waited while Turner wrestled with his conscience, the battle clearly showing on the man's face. "You just did your country a hell of a lot of good. Go the last step. Tell us what we need to know – what we're missing."

Turner looked up, blue eyes bright with something they hadn't had in a long time. "What I know is little to nothing ... but ... let me work with someone who *is* an engineer and maybe we can piece it all together."

"That's the man I knew!" He waited as his friend's expression didn't agree. "Why the reluctance?"

"I joined with Robur to get away from war, maybe even to prevent it. If I give you what I learned, I'm handing the military a new weapon. It's counter to everything I prayed for and agonized over. I had hoped to keep it all to myself, what little I have. But now? It's not really a matter of good and evil, black and white, is it? If I can't or won't get the U.S. up to level with this technological monstrosity they built, how many will die?"

"Very likely a damn sight more than if we're on equal fighting terms with this Confederacy." His voice dropped to a low whisper. "Mankind loves to fight. It isn't right but it is what happens. Even if we take the higher ground, people like Milton or Hagen make us defend ourselves. Ours is not the time of peace. But maybe we can do our part now to make things better for our children."

Perhaps Hagen had been partially correct. "Got any? Children, that is?" Turner said with a little spark and a desperate need to talk of something sane.

"Not yet. I do have a gal in ..."

A bullet tore through Willey's waistcoat, spraying Turner with blood, and he fell forward into Turner's arms. The projectile had deflected away from Turner. As every sailor ran forward to defend their position, Turner seized Willey under the arms and pulled him around the corner, into the shadows.

"Ah, Christ, Tom? No one tells you ... it hurts."

"Shut up, Ben. Let me see how bad it is."

"So much for this shirt. You ... you know I ... paid six dollars to have ... it made." He sounded weaker. "I'd like not ... to die now."

Pulling the waistcoat and the rather fine shirt open, Turner could see the bullet hole, surrounded with a puddle of red. It was bleeding profusely. He pulled a handkerchief out of Willey's pocket and pressed down on the wound. "Don't move."

"Figures. You warned ... me. Turner's Luck. You ... didn't get shot. Finish this fight. Beat them back."

Turner stared at his friend. How was it everyone around him got shot, or wounded, or harmed, but not him? It wasn't right. He looked again, lifting the handkerchief slightly, in case the wound was still pumping out blood. It was bad but not gushing, and he pressed the cloth down again, smiling in that lopsided way he did. "I'll leave finishing this to you."

"I'm dying."

Turner lowered his head until it touched the back of his own hand, pressing down on the wound. Then he began to laugh. Never out loud but with a good rumbling chuckle.

"I'm dying and ... you're ... you're laughing?"

Shaking his head, he looked at his friend. "The Turner Luck seems to have rubbed off on you. You may feel like hell right now, but that wound is through your shoulder, under the collar bone. I'm more worried about stopping the bleeding. But, I think you'll live."

Two shots ricocheted off the wall above their heads. Turner covered Willey's body with his own and waited for a break in the shots. A volley opened up on the sniper's position but after a minute, the sniper shot back, from a different location. He was moving around agilely. Probably one of Hagen's crew.

Two more officers arrived and began inspecting their comrade. By the time each had taken a look, even Willey seemed amused at his dumb luck. "You've lost a lot of blood there, Commander. But I think your friend here is right. You don't get to die today."

Willey waived unenthusiastically with his good arm. "Houghtaling ... get those men organized ... or that sniper will be picking them off next. Mac? Go get me ... something to clean up." Both men stared at Willey as though he were mad, if temporarily. "Move! I'm not going anywhere."

Grabbing Turner and pulling him closer, Willey cringed at the pain. "He's shooting at you." He took a deep breath of air. "Maybe you ... you were right. You're dangerous ... to be around."

"You may be stuck with me now."

Willey shook his head as much as he could and any torque on his shoulder clearly induced pain. His face tightened: his eyes closed. "Disappear. Now. Send me word … when you're … safe." He began shaking. The blood loss was not nearly as bad as the sheer pain. "No one … can hide you … like you can. I …" He began breathing heavily.

Turner looked again at the wound. It wasn't bleeding nearly so much. But he understood what it must feel like for the man who had been a clerk and occasionally a spy – who had never really known combat for what it was. "I don't want to just leave."

The sailors, with Houghtaling in the lead, burst from their positions and chased down the street. They'd sighted the sniper and were after him.

Turner watched. "That was too easy."

"Your luck … won't hold for me a second time. Go. I have people … they'll get me … on my feet." He grasped Turner's collar, looked hard at the scar on the man's neck, and considered in a fleeting second how brave a man would have to be to face death like that. He hurt, God how he hurt, but he knew he would probably live. What had Turner faced that could even compare to an experience of his? "I trust you. You came back. Go now. You won't … fail me."

As Mac arrived back with two seamen, a stretcher of sorts, and a Lieutenant with some knowledge of field medicine, they found Willey breathing painfully, but breathing. The man he was talking to had gone.

Despite the Commander's insistence to leave the man alone, Mac decided that Willey was reasonably incapacitated and put the order out to find this man. The Commander conveniently slipped unconscious before the name of the hunted man could be provided.

December 1883
Washington City
United States of America

The lady of the house paid the messenger for the telegram plus a small gift to compensate him for coming out in the dreadful winter snows so quickly. The boy wasn't from the Navy and any effort he made truly was above and beyond the requirements of duty. An enlisted naval messenger would have been given a cup of coffee, appropriately laced with something quite adult. The child, possibly ten or eleven years old, scampered off down the road, stopping to play in the snow on the side of the street the way all such boys should.

Waving off the maid, she climbed the stairs to her husband's study, where *they* were already meeting. She was one of the three wives allowed entrance without knocking or checking to see if the discussion was sensitive in nature and not for her civilian ears. Proudly she popped open the door and quickly shut it behind her.

The retired American Admiral paid virtually no attention – he was used to her prowling around his meetings and office. He even promised himself not to be surprised if one day, looking out at the latest Annapolis graduates, he espied his wife standing amongst the ensigns.

Nodding to the Admiral's wife and then to the Admiral, a gentleman with a pair of pale gray eyes looked up from a set of formal dispatches held in one hand, a cigar in the other. Without grinning too much, he said, "We're never getting away from this life are we?" His voice was gravelly and most sentences ended in a sharp cough.

"You can always head home, Mr. President, and I promise we'll say you were never here." The Admiral winked.

"And leave this all to you three?" When the Admiral's wife looked annoyed at him, he corrected the count to "four."

There were indeed four men and one woman in the room – meeting in relative secret. The Admiral and his wife; the gray-eyed former President; a fellow seated by the window; and a man lounging on the couch.

The fellow seated at the window, using the bright winter light to read by, called over with a thick Swedish accent, "Even more, if you count Julia."

"True. She'll want to be counted even when I'm not here anymore." The former President took a long drag on his cigar.

Seated in front of the fireplace, taking up most of the sofa with the long length of his body, the last man waved a hand dismissively. He stretched himself in a twist to see the others over his shoulder. Ginger red hair, fading in a few places, and dark hazel eyes. "Need I say six," he grumbled out in vague reference to his own wife.

"Dear God in Heaven," the Admiral whispered, staring at the telegram his wife had delivered. "He's survived... again."

"The man you're looking for," the Swede inquired, leaving his post at the window.

"The very same. He must have the damnedest luck."

"Or skill."

"Or both. Seems he stumbled upon our new friends in San Francisco. Got aboard their latest technological monstrosity and nearly destroyed it. They'll be in hiding for a bit, but I doubt they'll stay quiet for long. He gave our agent information about a ... a ..." God knew how much he hated the words coming out of his mouth. "... A new Confederacy. Do these individuals have nothing better to occupy their time but to try and revive a war they're too feckless to admit they lost? Now it seems they have a few oversized toys and heads full of idiotic ideas. Well ... he certainly gave good details about all of it – a thick report is on its way. Gives us a better chance from the start."

The red-head stood up from the couch. "I'm beginning to like the man. But couldn't the damn *Seches* come up with a better name." Seeing the Admiral's wife. "Please excuse my language, Ma'am. I'm tired of sitting and waiting for these fools to cause trouble before we can get the politicians to do something."

She didn't blink. "You damn well should. Admiral, I'll go get us some coffee." And with that, she strutted out the door.

"Thank you, Mrs. Admiral," he called after her, unashamed of the silly names they used for each other. The Admiral then smiled at the red-head. "She's been spending time with *your* wife, learning all sorts of bad habits."

The cigar smoker didn't look up. "You both like it and the sooner you admit you'd never want a docile wife, the better." Carefully, he set down the cigar, stifled a cough, and laid out the documents. "Gentlemen, we've known this day was coming. All the resentment from the South. Reconstruction gone wrong despite the best intentions. The North has to take some of the blame for it, no escaping that truth. No, this has been coming and now it's here. We need proof but it sounds like we may know just the man to get it for us."

"You thinking of bringing him back into the fold?"

"Why not, Admiral?"

"I don't like what he did for the past decade or so."

"We've all done things in the past that we don't brag about. None of us ever betrayed our country and it would appear the same is true for this fellow. Perhaps I should take a trip out west ..." The cigar smoker began to cough in earnest this time.

The red-head walked around the sofa with a deeply worried look on his face. Resting his hand on the smoker's shoulder, he offered, "No, that will be too obvious. I'll go. I have to do my tours of the forts as scheduled. A side trip won't be suspect. Besides, I want to meet this man."

"You should," the Swede noted. "After all, you're the one who saved his life."

The Capital proudly served coffee, sandwiches, and oysters to anyone able to afford the upper deck. In the winter, they diverted expended steam from the engines through pipes under the carpets, making the excursion up from the San Francisco and San Pablo bays much more of a pleasure. Below the highest deck, the pipes tended to drip water onto the less wealthy passengers. Thanks to a well stocked bar, few really cared.

Depending on the weather, availability of porters, and the speed at which one consumed their meal, the First Class travelers on the paddle-wheel ferry disembarked either first or last. Often, the well kept passengers waited and watched to see who was arriving and who was departing. Still, *The Capital* was required to keep a solid schedule and her captain wanted extra time to navigate the fast moving waters of the Sacramento River. She would barely get round trip and back into her home port by midnight as it was.

The last passenger was shooed down the gangplank by the purser and out into the rowdy river front. It was nothing compared to the Barbary Coast but it could be dangerous enough.

Sharply dressed, perfectly detailed, and moving without a single care as one might expect a well-to-do gentleman to stroll, though he had only a rail ticket and twenty dollars left in his pocket, the passenger sauntered along the raised boardwalks avoiding the mud and peered into several shop windows, careful to imply that he was in no hurry at all. Such a pace hid his limp too. His leg hurt still.

It was evening and the steamship had brought him to the central transportation hub of Sacramento exactly on time. He might have only thirty minutes to stretch and pose in his disguise before his train left for Denver.

Was it a disguise? He felt rather comfortable. Neatly shaven and wearing his excellent suit, he felt quite normal – as normal as he would in rolled up sleeves and well-worn boots.

He'd made some purchases that were necessary but almost too dear for his pocket. A walnut cane with a solid steel head. Oh, it was as shiny as any silver plated tea set at the Palace Hotel, yet it needed to be stronger by far – it was his first weapon, readily in hand. A good piece of luggage, big enough to store five cases of ammunition and two Colt pistols along with a growing number of disguises. A heavy wool overcoat. A double-sided knife that fit neatly in the pocket he'd sewn inside his sleeve. A small valise in which to carry basic gentleman's goods, a half filled but lately ignored journal, a paper-wrapped selection of dried meat and jerked beef, a small chemical lantern from Hawai'i, a .32 caliber Derringer, and a false set of correspondence on rather expensive paper intended to complete his disguise as a businessman. *The letter* he now kept in a pouch he purchased from a man selling "western" trinkets to the tourists. As was the style of imitated Indian bags, this was made of elk hide and hung by a cord he adjusted so that it put her letter over his heart. No one would see that unless he was dead.

Gentleman or not, Turner had to compensate for appearances with practicality. His ticket was for second class, and he was not likely to be alone. The difference between first and second class was an outrageous twenty-five dollars and many travelling "gentlemen" and "occupied gentlemen" saved their nickels by accepting the discomforts of the lower class travel.

The Central Pacific Railroad's locomotive #252 chugged backward until it bumped into the crew car, hitching the two together, and narrowly missing the switchman who monitored all the couplings. The man darted between the cars and set the pins that would hold everything together. Once done, he waved to the engineer and ran to the next car to repeat the process.

It was a job Turner was glad he didn't have. He sauntered to the end of the passenger boardwalk to look at the engine. The Central Pacific Railroad, CPRR, #252 was new, but hardly close to the technological marvels he'd seen and known. For once it was satisfying to see something normal, something time honored and tested, something so simple a child – with enormous strength – could handle. The engine was low and wide, painted in a spectacular shade of red, with black filigree detailing. While not particularly tall, it had a broad smoke stack that was usual for wood-burning locomotives yet it had a strong smell of coal. That was comforting, considering the locomotive he'd seen earlier. With any luck that extraordinary piece of equipment had been apprehended by Commander Willey and was no longer a threat. Tuner felt the cold air more sharply than before while he considered how unlikely that was.

The CPRR did indeed give the train a technological advantage: it provided remarkably strong lights via chemical interaction for the engine's headlamp and the engineer's cab lights. They seemed brighter by far than his little lantern but that was just as well, he thought. And, it was rumored that the CPRR had invested in five track clearing trains that used a tremendous amount of fuel to generate high-pressure steam jets to remove any snow or ice that could impede the transit. Turner was hoping to see such a machine in action.

The conductor called for all to board. Precisely timed. The train was set to leave at 8:50 in the evening. That late in the year, the sun had long since set and a deep chill was settling over the city. It had snowed the week before but it had turned to rain and then to clear skies. The river was swollen and the ground muddy, but that didn't eliminate the wishes of every child, and perhaps Turner too, that there could be fluffy white snow to make forts from.

He gladly passed the elegant Pullman Palace car and, after assisting a lady in a loud green plaid bustle suit first, climbed up into the fourth car from the front. Second class was busy but agreeable. It seemed the chemical lights had caught on, possibly due to the notion that gas lights were difficult and open flame not recommend for wooden passenger cars. There was no way yet to avoid the coal stoves at either end of the car which provided the only source of desperately needed heat; should something happen, the chance of the car being engulfed in flame was extremely high.

Turner lifted his luggage case to the rope hammock above his seat, certain that someone's baggage was going to overwhelm the overhead storage and cause it to come crashing down. His valise he would keep handy, if for no other reason than for a makeshift pillow. His seat was a two man bench, cushioned in a nice, busy-patterned, utilitarian fabric, and he had the laudable ability to open and close his window. It would be six hours to Colton Station, Truckee, and another day and a half to Denver via Cheyenne– *if* the tracks were clear. He was travelling in December and taking a terrible chance with the weather. If he was lucky, and he was Lucky Tom Turner, he would have the entire bench to himself.

No such luck tonight. A nervous man sat down next to him, stared at him with big almost frightened eyes hiding behind wire-rim glasses, mopped his gleaming brow, and clutched a small bag to his chest as if it would protect him from robbers and women with equal effect. A waft of pungent flowers followed him on the air. He was perfumed. Interesting, Turner thought.

It was probably better to not scare the fellow, Turner decided, and he merely gave the man a polite, silent, nod. The man flicked his head up and down, then stared forward until the train began its halting, bone jarring pick up from stop to top speed. Coming out of the Sacramento rail yard, the entire train rocked and swayed, reminding anyone with travel experience of a rough sea voyage. Some woman behind him commented as much, quite stridently. If only she knew what flying the *Albatross* through a typhoon was like, he thought, she'd have little to complain about.

The man next to him squirmed but kept his eyes tightly shut. Turner took a moment to study him. About a hand and a half shorter than him, the man was around thirty-five in age, pale sandy-haired, wearing a dark blue sack suit of wool and a knitted scarf wrapped around his throat twice. His hands were surprisingly strong for such a delicately built fellow, and manicured. He had the overall appearance of man easily keeping his financial head well above water, with a wife and numerous children somewhere east of the Rockies, and maintaining his work routine in the hopes he might survive until a comfortable retirement and always to brag of his success in an oblique manner. He did smell of gardenias which was somewhat incongruent with the rest of him. Out of one sleeve appeared a silver and gem-stone cuff stud and the edge of a linen handkerchief. His hair was oiled but that did not straighten the tight curls bounding from his high forehead. His eyes were deeply sunken and round, reminding one more of a pug dog than a human.

Turner looked away before he might be caught staring, and watched the odd glow from the locomotive's headlamp touching every tree and bush as they rushed by. It would be mid morning at the earliest before they would arrive in Reno. Passengers would have a brief time to stretch their legs and, for second class passengers, a chance to purchase breakfast. Dinner was served in first class only –

everyone else was left to their own devices.

The last cheroot cigar from his pocket was pleasant – too much so. Surely he should break himself of the habit, but every bit of tobacco was vaunted as being either healthful or mannered, for what man would go without? Somehow, he thought while drawing in the sweetened smoke, he couldn't help but wonder at how effectively gentlemen were being manipulated. Including himself, he considered fairly.

The train jostled through a narrow canyon of snow created by the removal engines. He hadn't had the pleasure of seeing them working in the deep Sierra woods, but one had rumbled through Truckee blowing away some minor snowpack from the town center. Multiple jets of directed steam blasted out from beneath the locomotive, melting the snow near it and galvanizing the pack into substantial ice some two meters away on either side. The ice would melt slowly, well clear of the tracks. In town, the engine moved slowly and at less than half its capacity. Out on the meandering tracks headed into Reno, it would be a splendid sight filled with vaporized snow and solidified ice.

There was one certain thing: the New Confederate's revolutionary locomotive would be hindered just as easily as any common engine, despite all the advances in design. Turner smiled at that thought. Nature would always win. He leaned back on the swaying car, planting his feet firmly on the boarding platform for balance.

The door opened and Turner's bench mate stepped through, carefully shutting the door as if it were entirely made of glass. He seemed more fussy than usual. Hands were jammed under his coat arms and he sniffed unhappily at the cold air. Looking up at Turner, he managed a slight smile. "Good evening, sir. Would you have a match?"

Placing his cigarillo in his mouth, Turner quickly rummaged in his coat pocket for the book of matches he'd just used. Glancing up and holding the book out, he took immediate interest in the snub nosed, matte black, ugly gun pointed at him. All he could muster was a raised eyebrow and an exhausted, lopsided grin. His hand had only seconds before touched on the Derringer in his pocket.

"If you will please put your hands above your head." It was half question, half demand.

This was not Turner Luck, or was it? After taking his cigarillo in one hand, he raised both half heartedly. "I'm not particularly flush?"

"Oh no, Mr. Turner, I am not interested in your money. I work for a certain employer and his remuneration is much more satisfying. Please keep your hands there. I am going to search your pockets."

"You know my name?" Oh no.

"I have been following you for some time, making inquiries. You are a difficult man to find, Mr. Turner." The fellow's accent was European, but neither British, German, nor French.

"I don't suppose you'd be willing to tell me who sent you?"

"Monsieur Pierre-Jules Hetzel of Paris. I believe you know him?"

Turner's good humor faded immediately and it showed on his face. He was not entirely certain why he would have preferred New Confederates at that moment. Perhaps it was because he preferred dealing with the situation human to human, not human to half-machine. He allowed the little man to scour his coat lining and pockets. Looking for an opening, none came and the man removed the derringer with satisfaction. "So. You're enhanced? What did Hetzel fix on you?"

"No." He drew the word out for some length of time, seeming to be a bit astonished at Turner's assumption. "No. No. I'm just a man who collects things … oh, and people, yes. I collect those too."

"Collects and kills?" His voice registered too much disgust.

"Ah … you don't know." Now the little man was overjoyed at having something Turner wanted. "This is too charming. You are completely unaware of the change?"

"Pardon me? As things have come to pass, I'm not in much of a humor to see the joke." He wanted to drop his hands. His coat was heavy and tight on his arms and the feeling was ebbing from his fingers. The man was maintaining a safe distance, making the hidden knife useless.

"Monsieur Hetzel of Paris, my employer, has changed his interest in the nature of your future well-being. You are to be captured, not killed, though if you give me too much difficulty, I will have to resort to extreme measures against you, Mr. Turner. I promise it is nothing personal; it is only a matter of business. I won't be compensated nearly as much if I send a corpse to Monsieur Hetzel. But please, Mr. Turner, do not underestimate me and do not try my patience."

He chewed on his lower lip for a moment, trying not to smile. "I'm too exhausted to make much of this and too curious not to ask more. Just how do you propose to get me to Hetzel in France? Don't worry, I'm not going to wrestle with you, I'm too intrigued by all this. May I put my hands down?"

"Only if you give me your word you won't try to take this gun from me?"

"To whom am I giving my word?" Turner lowered his hands and slipped them into his warm pockets. Empty pockets.

"Oh, you can call me Mr. Cairo, Mr. Heinrich Cairo. That is a place in Egypt."

Turner grinned. "I'm aware of that. I've been there. Have you?"

Cairo shook his head. "Never. But that is hardly the point. I do wish we could go inside but our conversation mustn't be overheard." He wisely stepped back from Turner. "Monsieur Hetzel, my employer …"

"… we've established that …"

"… wishes me to present you with an offer. It is his belief that you have become, shall we say, a bit too expensive to oppose, yet he is concerned that your knowledge of certain endeavors of his puts his business and country at risk. He does not wish to seem rude, but you are clearly not in support of his developments and activities."

"Let's shorten this, Mr. Cairo. Hetzel believes that I will tell the world he is making mechanical monstrosities out of natural men and he wants assurances I won't do that."

Cairo nodded, thinking his more colorful and vague description was better. "If you come with me to meet him, I believe you will be able to arrange a mutually satisfying agreement."

His hands sank deeply into his pockets. "Or he'll kill me.

Doesn't that bother you, even a little?"

The little man shook his head and looked a bit annoyed at the question. "Not at all. Frankly, I would find it much easier to bring you back in a box than to spend the trip worried about what you might do next. As I said, I will be paid just perhaps a touch less." He took a step forward and leveled the gun. "Now, obviously, I cannot deal with you in a crowded car. You will please remove your hands from your pockets, so that I may see them, and lead the way to the livestock car. Be assured, I am a very good shot."

Removing his hands and noting that the freezing air did not make them feel colder – they were already frozen – he turned to the gap between the cars, ready to move into the Third Class car and further to the back of the train. He could do nothing with people surrounding them. Admiral Hagen was right about his weaknesses.

As though reading Turner's thoughts, Cairo came up behind him closely. "I am not afraid of shooting anyone who gets in my way or will offer you assistance, so perhaps we can just leave them out of it? I am certain you do not want any of those poor innocent people harmed?"

"You're a coward, you know that. And I'm sick to death of nasty little men like you using innocent lives to cower behind!"

"That was uncalled for," Cairo said, genuinely shocked and offended.

New Confederates and Prussian admirals slaughtered the men at Fort Point and had every intention of using the populace of Mexico to shield their activities. The pirates in Hawaii did the same. He'd seen it time and time again. Innocent people dragged into the affairs of people who claimed to know better. Lives destroyed. Hopes obliterated for greed and power. Turner's whole body shook with a rage of it, and every drop of that fury flowed into the fist he slammed into Cairo's nose.

The little man dropped both guns and protected his nose, squealing in anger and hurt. "Look what you've done!"

"How about ..." he didn't finish the sentence until he'd struck the man in the face again, knocking him to the platform, "... this?" Grabbing the half sensible Cairo by the collar, he lifted the man up. The fellow weighed very little. Ahead the train whistle began blowing: they were coming into a town. He knew there was no stop and the train's continued speed confirmed this. But the whistle had to be blown at certain junctions so that a signal could be sent by telegraph wire that the train and her passengers had passed by safely. Why he cared or desired to be merciful, Turner never understood but gratefully accepted as one of his few good points – or failings.

Pulling Cairo over to the side of the platform, with the whole train swaying and rocking, he held him near the safety rail. "Listen to me, Mr. Cairo. I am not going to France; alone, with you, or with anyone else. I don't give a goddamn about Hetzel and his monstrosities."

"Your language, sir ..."

He yanked the little man up against the rail, leaning him dangerously over it. "Tell Hetzel to leave me the hell alone. I have no intention of telling the world anything. But if he persists, not only will I send every one of his agents home in a box or in pieces, I *will* go to the press with one of them as an example. Do you understand your *new* instructions, Mr. Cairo?"

"Please don't send me back in pieces! I will tell Monsieur Hetzel what you are saying. I will assure him of your ... sincerity."

Turner let go of him and let his feet settle back on the platform. The little man started by straightening his collar, blotting his nose with the lace handkerchief and combing back his hair. "That was not necessary. It was very rude in fact."

"You threatened to use civilians as shields."

He quickly drew another small pistol out of his handkerchief pocket. "And I will again, as it seems so very important to you. Now, you will place your hands on your head and ..."

Turner hit him so hard that he had no conscious awareness of tumbling over the rail and into the snow. He only cleared his pounding head when an ill dressed man assisted him to his feet, welcomed him to some town too small to have a memorable name, and promptly arrested him for being apparently too drunk to stay on the train. Protesting all the way to the one and only jail cell for 50 miles, Cairo prayed that this food-stain-on-a-map would have a telegraph line he could use. When his head stopped hurting.

Turner had purposefully not bothered to care where Cairo fell, though before he went inside, he begrudgingly looked out at the town and thought he might have seen Cairo being assisted to his feet. Fine … he did care, regardless of Cairo's own misconduct.

Dropping into his seat, he realized with no small amount of satisfaction that he wouldn't have to share the bench. And now he had three pistols: his own derringer returned and the two Cairo had pulled on him.

It was sloppy of him, and he knew he couldn't afford to be sloppy, but he felt nearly invincible. No … he felt entirely invincible. Even a bit smug. Hetzel was giving up. Thousands of miles away from Paris, Hetzel was ineffective. Machines, enhanced creatures, pirates, ghosts, Crimps, Confederates and Prussians … Hetzel had sent them all to kill poor old Tom Turner. He folded his arms and allowed himself to settle back in his cushioned seat, turning his body slightly to take advantage of the empty seat next to him. He closed his eyes, honestly acknowledging that this was not a good idea for a man on the run … on the defensive.

He was on the offensive. He'd made up his mind and stayed true to his course. He was winning and though he knew he shouldn't have, he was feeling cocky. He was even considering if it was safe enough to seek out Lettie Gantry?

The smoke from the wood stove gave the car a pungent yet oddly pleasant smell and with that, Turner allowed himself to fall asleep. Not, however, before he settled one hand over his pocket derringer.

Someone who smoked cigars, had entered Turner's room without permission and was waiting for him. The sun had just set behind the mountains, cutting Denver off from an extra hour of light that the rest of the country enjoyed. The light was still strong outside but it left deep, enlarged shadows in the corners.

Reflexively, Turner drew the larger revolver he'd kept from the Cairo mishap out across his torso and held it close to his body. He entered the room cautiously, turning his side to the bulk of the room so that he offered the narrowest of targets. It had been a long time since he'd encountered a threat, yet he remained constantly alert for trouble.

A slight squeaking of the rocking chair's runners kept rhythmically moving. The unbidden visitor was seated near the window and taking advantage of the only seat in the room. The silhouette showed a man, quietly waiting.

The figure turned toward him. "Shall we put up the light?" The voice was husky, probably from too many years of smoking and drinking.

Turner reached over to the gas toggle, clicking it twice to create the spark for the light above his bed, then increased the flow of gas to amplify the brightness.

He kept his revolver at the ready.

The man looking at him was especially unique. A pale beard covered most of his face; lighter nearest the muzzle and darker toward the sideburns and jaw. A darker red – though the gray and white had overwhelmed most of it. The man still had a full, thick shock of ginger hair covering his head, despite the fact that he was clearly in his sixties and should have been balding or entirely white-headed like other men his age. Tall. By far taller than Turner and taller than most men. And rail thin. Once standing, Turner could see that the man's shoulders were squared and his posture superior. A military man.

Turner knew the face though he'd never spoken a word to him before this moment. His revolver sank until it was pointed at the floor. "Sir?"

"Turner? It's about time we met."

Words escaped him. Turner stood there, dumbstruck.

"Don't sailors talk? I'm told army men can't shut up – well, perhaps they just meant me." The man had a twinkle in his hazel eyes, now that they weren't wondering what might happen with the gun that had been pointed at him.

"General?" Turner found one appropriate word.

"Good. You know two words. Think you can produce a sentence? How about an answer?"

"To what question, sir?"

"Where the hell do you keep the whiskey? Two men shouldn't sit and talk of old times without something to drink. Old times *and* new times. I think you may have some interesting new times ahead of you."

The Turner Luck held true.

Along with feeling he'd finally beaten Hetzel, now he was getting a long held wish fulfilled. His world could not have been better in that moment. It was a sign that his life had turned a corner and would be just fine. "General W. T. Sherman, I presume?"

Date unknown, 1884
March?
A Tombstone Mine, Arizona Territory

Freezing water

Death had been chasing Turner and now had caught up. His fingertips went numb. So too did his feet. His lungs burned. There was little difference between this and being strangled ... hanged ...

... It was over ...

His life ... oh God what a life he'd led ...

... It was over ...

... No! He had to live!

He had to survive. He had to see Lettie one more time. He couldn't die like this. He had piloted and commanded Robur's airship. He'd beaten Monsieur Hetzel at the game of assassination. He'd survived Andersonville. He was his father's son and the only living soul to remember the man's name with honor.

The box slid again, this time leaving only the tiniest space of air. Sound drowned into a horrible sloshing and bubbling: the pressure of the water tightened around his ears. Filthy water filled his nose, leaving a stench inside.

His body shaking and becoming numb, he had one last chance – one last try. He pushed himself up to the pocket of air, filled his chest as much as possible, and dropped underneath the water. One more try – One last try -

THE YANKEE MUST DIE

THE GASLIGHT ADVENTURES OF TOM TURNER

Terror in the Wild Weird West
COMING SOON

Also coming soon: don't miss the continuing saga of
Dr. Lettie Gantry
in

The Volcano Lady – Volume 3:

THE GREAT EARTHQUAKE MACHINE

ABOUT THE AUTHOR

T. E. MacArthur is an author, artist, and historian living in the San Francisco Bay Area with her constant companion, Mac the cat. She received her Bachelor's Degree in History from Cal State University and spent many an evening in subsequent Anthropology, Geology, Criminal Investigation and Art classes. Writing, however, remains her passion. She has written for several local and specialized publications and was even an accidental sports reporter for Reuters with three national bi-lines.

The Volcano Lady: Volumes I & II follow the adventures of Victorian lady scientist Lettie Gantry. *The Yankee Must Die* novellas continue the thrilling adventures of Tom Turner following the time honored cliffhangers of dime novels, penny dreadfuls, and weekly serials. To put it mildly, T.E. has a love for all things Victorian (history and clothing from 1870 – 1890 in particular) and is having a lifelong affair with the writings of Jules Verne.

VISIT T. E. MACARTHUR ON HER BLOG:
http://volcanolady1.wordpress.com

OR ON FACEBOOK:
https://www.facebook.com/pages/The-Volcano-Lady-by-TE-MacArthur/137109946299830

www.ingramcontent.com/pod-product-compliance
Lightning Source LLC
Chambersburg PA
CBHW020250150626
46552CB00020B/751